A DOLLAR'S

Al was sitting in a booth with Sally. He was staring at a man who had been peering avidly at Sally's very short shorts.

The man at the bar got up to leave and Leeds said, "You owe the lady a dollar, Mister."

The man turned. "What for?"

"I figure you got a dollar's worth of fun out of staring at her legs. Pay her." He grabbed the man's arm.

The man hesitated and Leeds tightened his grip, his eyes hooded and dangerous. The man put his hand in his pocket and threw a dollar on the table. Leeds let him go and he walked quickly out of the bar.

Sally said, "What'd you do that for?"

"I wanted to scare him out of a dollar."

She stared at him for a moment, then she began to laugh. . . .

AUTHOR'S PROFILE

Glenn Canary was born in Bowling Green, Kentucky, but spent his early years in Massillon, Ohio. He is a graduate of Ohio State University where he majored in literature and psychology.

After college he became a salesman and buyer for a chain of department stores, then shifted to the Massillon EVE-NING INDEPENDENT as a news reporter, covering everything from football games to murders and weddings. He is currently working in the book club department of Doubleday & Company.

His stories have appeared in Gent, Dude, Manhunt, Modern Man and Ed McBain's Mystery Magazine. He is the author of the Monarch bestselling novel entitled THE DAMNED AND THE INNOCENT.

CURRENT BESTSELLING MONARCH BOOKS

A Contemporary Novel

THE TRAILER PARK GIRLS

Glenn Canary

Author of THE DAMNED AND THE INNOCENT

Women Of The World Fiction Series

MONARCH BOOKS, INC.

Derby, Connecticut

THE TRAILER PARK GIRLS

A Monarch Books Original Novel

Published in April, 1962

Copyright © 1962 by Glenn Canary

Cover Painting by Harry Barton

Monarch books are published by MONARCH BOOKS, INC., Capital Building, Derby, Connecticut, and represent the works of outstanding novelists and writers of non-fiction especially chosen for their literary merit and reading entertainment.

Printed in the United States of America

CHAPTER 1

The jukebox slurred to a stop.

Burt Stone straightened up and dropped the cord to the floor. He walked back to the bar and began to sort bottles.

"Hey, what the hell's going on?" the man at the bar said. "I paid to hear that record. What the hell you doing turning off the music?"

"I'm closing this place," Stone said. "You've played that record a dozen times and you're drunk. I've already waited half an hour for you to finish your drink."

"Who the hell's drunk?" the man said. "Turn the goddamn music on."

"Finish up and shove off. I'm closed up."

"Who's drunk? If you wasn't back of that bar, I'd show you who's drunk."

Stone turned his back and opened the cash register. He was a slender man of medium height and his black hair and light skin didn't seem to go together.

"Come on, you," the drunk said, "turn the goddamn music back on. I paid to hear it."

Stone turned to look at him. "Get out of here," he said. "You're drunk and I'm sick of listening to you."

The man stood up. He had to brace himself against the bar. "You're a big man, aren't you?" he said. "You're so big I think I'll just come back there and fix myself a drink on the house and see how you like that." He leaned over the bar and pointed at Stone.

"You come over here and I'll break you in half," Stone said softly.

"Why don't you get a cop, big man? Why don't you call for help? See if the cops don't make you turn the goddamn music back on."

"All right," Stone said. He came around the end of the bar. "I told you, lush."

The drunk backed away, his hands in front of him. "Come

5

on," he said. "Come on, big man. Show me what a big man a bartender is."

Stone stepped close to him. The drunk punched wildly, but Stone only shrugged and let it bounce off his shoulder. He grabbed the man's arm and spun him around and kneed him in the buttocks. "Get going, buddy," he grunted.

The drunk was still yelling when he landed on his face on the sidewalk. When he sat up, his nose was bleeding. Stone waited in the doorway to see what he would do, but he stood up, weaving, and began to walk away, still cursing.

Stone started to go back into the bar and he saw Jack Cannon and Al Leeds waiting for him in Cannon's car. He waved at them and went in, locking the door behind him.

He picked up a chair that had been knocked over and slammed it back against a table. At the bar, he took a rag and cleaned off the top of the counter quickly and then went to the register to check out the money. He knew Louis, who owned the place, would be in at eight in the morning to take the money from the safe and deposit it in the bank.

It had been a good night. There were three hundred dollars in the till. He counted it and then stood with the bills in his hand, looking at them. Most of the money hadn't been rung up; he didn't have time for that when he got busy. He thought Louis probably suspected he was taking some. He could take as much as a hundred tonight. Louis wouldn't even suspect that there was anywhere near three hundred dollars there.

He swore and slipped the money into the safe. Somebody was going to crack that safe some night, but that wasn't any of his concern. He wouldn't be here then. He kicked the door shut and bent to lock it.

"Who the hell needs it?" he said aloud, still thinking of the money.

He was twenty-seven years old, but when he laughed then, he looked younger . . .

Burton Stone was twenty-one the day he picked up his diploma at New York University and quit his job at Macy's. The last five years had been hard and long, especially long because he had had to work so many hours that it took an extra year to graduate. But now he held the paper that said he was fit to enter medical school.

He was so happy that day that it didn't even sadden him that he had no family at the commencement exercises. For a few seconds he had been depressed. It seemed everyone had parents and brothers and sisters and aunts and uncles. But his only relative was a brother who couldn't take off from driving a cab just to see his kid brother graduate from college.

For a crazy few minutes he even thought of wearing his cap and gown while he went home on the subway.

His landlady came to his room when he got there. She said she wanted to wish him well. It wasn't too bad. Besides, he couldn't even remember his mother and his father's memory was beginning to fade.

And just then nothing mattered because he had his diploma, because he was ready to enter medical school, and because there was ten thousand dollars in the bank for him to use to pay for it. Ten thousand dollars. His share of the twenty thousand in insurance his father had left.

It had been hard not to use that money. But a man could work his way to a bachelor's degree. It was tough, but not impossible as it would be in medical school. So he hadn't used it and it was there, waiting.

Only, of course, it wasn't there at all.

When they told him at the bank he ran the eighteen blocks to his brother's apartment. He ran hard all the way and when he got there, he was panting and crying and he couldn't talk. He stood there beside his brother's dinner table with his brother's kids watching the tears that were running down his face. Mary, his brother's wife, got up and left the room. All she said was, "I told you."

"So what the hell's the matter with you?" his brother said.

"That was my money," he was able to say. "That was my money."

"So who needed it worse? Me with three kids or a young kid without no responsibility? Besides, I only borrowed it."

"I want it back."

7

"It ain't there to get back."

"It can't be all gone."

His brother laughed sharply. "The hell it can't."

"What did you do with it?"

"I put it into the liquor store."

"The liquor store," he screamed. "That was my money."

"Can I help it the store went bust? How the hell you think I feel? You think I wanted to lose your money or something? I was going to give it back to you with interest."

Then suddenly all the anger was gone out of him. He sat down in a chair and looked at the pork roast on the table. "What am I going to do now?" he said.

"Go to work," his brother said. "Get yourself a job. You got a degree now. Get yourself into some outfit as a trainee."

"I wanted to be a doctor."

"You better get yourself a job."

"You owe me that money."

"Of course," his brother said, "you may not have much to say about it. You'll probably get drafted pretty quick."

Stone never forgot what came next. Even when he got older and was able to see that his brother really did aim to build a business and pay him back, even then he wasn't able to forget.

He said, "Why didn't you ask me first? What gave you the right to use my money?"

"I never even thought about it," his brother said.

Two weeks later Burton Stone joined the army. Of course he realized before he was through with basic training that he had done something stupid.

But when his enlistment ran out, he didn't know what else to do, so he enlisted again.

But maybe it wasn't so bad. The army did toughen him up. The very first time he had leave he went back to New York and clubbed his brother right in the mouth.

Then he turned and walked away. He remembered better than anything the way his brother just sat there on the floor, his lip split and bleeding, and didn't say anything or make any move to get up until after Stone left the apartment.

In the army, too, he met Jack Cannon and Al Leeds. He was the one who first thought seriously of the plan, but it was Leeds' specific information that led them to pick Columbus, Ohio, and the big department store in the Graceland Shopping Center.

He still wanted to be a doctor, now worse than ever. He had worked in the medical corps in the army, but that wasn't enough. And he figured that he had ten thousand dollars coming.

He aimed to get it . . .

They were waiting for him when he left the bar. Leeds was driving. He started the engine as soon as Stone came out and eased it into gear and pulled up beside the front door to pick him up.

Stone climbed in and slammed the door heavily.

"Who's got a cigarette?"

Jack Cannon was in the back seat, sitting across it with his heavy legs on the seat. He tossed a pack of cigarettes across. "Why didn't you get some from that guy you threw out?"

"He didn't smoke my brand."

Leeds said, "We going to try it for time tonight?"

"Let's try it," Stone said. "Just don't attract attention."

"Nobody notices me but women," Leeds said.

"Man, you're your own best salesman," Cannon said. "You're so modest."

They all laughed.

"You guys are just jealous because I look like Marlon Brando."

"Sure," Stone said. "Everyone's jealous but Marlon."

"There's the store," Cannon said.

Stone leaned forward tensely. "All right. Pull up in front of it there in the parking lot and stop. Then start out and not too fast."

"Man," Leeds said. "I'm a regular old lady."

"We stop here," Stone said, "and you stay in the car with the motor running. Jack and I take the guns and go in for the money. Then we come out and get back in the car." He looked at his watch. "Okay. Now."

Leeds gunned the car out of the parking lot and onto North High Street.

"Watch the lights," Stone said. "Not too fast."

"I'll drive," Leeds said tightly.

In less than two minutes they were past the city limits and on open highway. Leeds leaned back and the car jumped ahead. "You need a carburetor adjustment," he said to Cannon.

"So I'll buy me a Cadillac when we're done."

"We'll pick one of these side roads to hide the car on," Stone said, musing. "Then we'll ditch the stolen car, switch to this one and be back in town by the time any roadblocks get set up."

"I wonder how much we'll get," Cannon said.

"I told you how much we'd get," Leeds answered.

"I know, but maybe your buddy who worked there was stretching it."

"He wasn't a buddy, just a fraternity brother, but he wasn't putting me on. He said any Saturday night there's between thirty and forty thousand dollars in there."

"And no cops?"

"No cops," Stone broke in. "I've watched. No one seems to think it's possible that police should be around that much money."

"And just two guys to take," Leeds said. "A manager and an assistant manager and they're under company orders not to resist a holdup. Let the insurance company worry about it."

"When are we going to do it?" Cannon asked.

Stone swiveled around to look at him. "We'll take our time. We want to make sure we have everything figured out, so don't push it."

"We're not pushing," Leeds said. He nosed the car into a side road and turned it around and started back. "We're just anxious."

"Slow down," Stone said. "This isn't a race."

Leeds swung the car east and picked up Westerville Road. After a few minutes of driving in silence, he said, "There's the trailer park where live those famous bandits, Frank, Jesse and Mortimer James."

He turned into the park and hit a six-inch high ridge in the driveway.

"Goddamn it," Stone said. "Why don't you ever remember those things?"

Leeds eased over the next bump. There was one every fifteen feet. "I still don't see why those silly bastards had to put them in anyway. Who can remember?"

"They put them in to slow us down when we come in here," Stone said.

Cannon laughed. "Everyone knows that anyone who lives in a trailer park is either a hillbilly or a cowboy. You're a cowboy, Al."

The trailer camp was shiny with metal under moonlight. Stone always thought it was funny the way people cleaned the trailers. There was also a large metal awning on nearly every one and most of them were surrounded by flowers. Once, out of idleness, he asked the owner of the trailer camp about his business and he received in return an embittered lecture.

"Everyone thinks we're riff-raff because we live in mobile homes," he said. "We can't even get charge accounts."

Stone laughed. "Don't they think you'll stay long enough?"

"Aw, it ain't that. They think everyone here is unsettled or something."

But they were unsettled, Stone saw after he had lived there awhile. The war did it. Trailers—mobile homes to those who live in them—were rare before the war, but after the war they appealed to the transient, to the bored, to the unemployed who thought there was more and better work somewhere else, to the unsettled. Nearly all the people there were working stiffs and many were decent individuals. But there were also the cowboys and the hard-looking women and the screaming voices you heard every night.

And despite the awnings and the flowers, every trailer was ready to roll. So were the people.

The plots of ground allotted to the trailers were small and Stone always thought the people looked ready to run.

11

They had a small home on a small piece of rented ground and their only contact with a stable society was the electric plug that socked into the side of the trailer when it was parked. The radios all were too loud. The cars were too flashy—even the old ones.

But that's why he wanted a trailer. No one looks at people who live in trailers.

They lived in a fifty-foot, aluminum Spartan trailer. When they reached it that night, a small light was burning at the door. The inside was panelled. At the front was a large green couch with a back that was built into the wall. Above that were bookcases. A table hung flat against one wall. The refrigerator was set into a nook. Across from that was a bottled gas stove. The sinks were aluminum. In the back of the trailer were two bedrooms. In the larger they had bunks, army style. In the smaller, they had a card table set up. On it was a map.

"Anybody want a beer?" Leeds said, opening the refrigerator.

"Sure," Cannon said.

Stone waved him away and went back to take a shower.

"Man," Leeds said, sitting down after opening beer, "I sure am looking forward to getting this over with. I'm tired of living like a monk. Have you seen some of the babes who live here?"

"Some monk." Cannon laughed. "And those babes would chew you up for breakfast."

"Right now," Leeds said, "I can't think of a better way to die."

They drank their beer and they were still laughing when Stone came back to see what all the noise was about.

CHAPTER 2

"What we try to do," Jack Cannon said, "is to work out an insurance plan that is designed specifically to fit your personal needs now and in the future."

"That makes sense," the man across the desk said.

"It would be easy enough to try to sell you a policy for twenty thousand dollars, but I'm interested in being your insurance contact for a long time. If you don't need it, I don't want to sell it to you."

The customer sat back. "Well," he said, "a man is always interested in providing a secure future for his family."

"I'll need to ask a few rather personal questions in order to determine exactly what your needs and problems are."

"All right, fire away."

"Now then, exactly when were you born . . . ?"

Jack Cannon was a big man. He was twenty-five years old, but it was hard to guess his age because he was of a type that is overpowering. He was over six feet tall and he weighed two hundred thirty pounds. He was proud of his body and of his physical condition and he had the big man's good-humored contempt or pity for small men. He had sandy-brown hair and his face was round and heavily bearded.

He had to have all his dress shirts made to measure because ready-made were too small in the arms for him. He laughed easily and he was not a stupid man even though he was flunked out of the University of Pittsburgh after his junior year. And he was one of the fortunate types who always seem to get just what they want by simply asking for it. Sometimes, too, he laughed at himself because the calendar of his life was neither Julian nor Gregorian, but Feminine.

Before fourteen, there was only time. What does anyone do before he is fourteen? He was born and raised in Massillon, Ohio, and his father owned a hardware store that earned enough to make the family moderately well-off by Massillon standards.

So his calendar started when he was fourteen and a freshman in high school. The first time period was also fourteen and her name was Alice Rankin. He went to see her one night because he had heard other boys talking about her. He found her on her porch, swinging, and waiting as if she had known he was coming.

"Hi," he said.

"Hi."

"What are you doing?"

"Swinging."

"I was just coming by."

"I saw you coming."

"You doing anything special?"

"Swinging." She laughed at him.

"You want to take a walk or something?"

"What something?" She laughed again, but she came down to the sidewalk to meet him.

They went for a walk down by the reservoir and he kissed her a few times. He was bumbling and she kept opening her mouth and he thought that was a hell of a thing, but it was nice anyway. They leaned against a tree and he touched her breasts outside her clothes. After a while she said, "I'm getting hot."

"What?" he said.

She didn't answer, but she took his right hand and put it inside her blouse. She leaned against him and moaned in her throat. At first he thought he was hurting her and he started to pull away, but she wouldn't let him go.

"Let's get away where it's darker," she said.

He didn't know what to do. He looked down toward the water, but he didn't move until she took his hand and began leading him further into the wooded area that stretched around toward Wales Spring where the older boys who had cars could take their dates.

She took him to a place that was around the curve of the reservoir and completely cut off from the sight of people in houses. Three evergreen trees were growing in a triangle and they stood in the deeper shadows there. It was too dark to see the ground, but it felt spongy and he thought there must be a thick layer of moss on it.

Alice put her arms around his neck again and began kissing him. Then she drew back a little, just far enough so she could look up into his face without releasing the pressure of her breasts against his chest. "I bet you'll tell other guys that I let you do this," she said.

"No, I won't."

"I'll bet you will." Her voice sounded suddenly distant and older.

14

"I won't," he said. "I promise I won't."

"Cross your heart you won't." She sounded like a little girl again.

He made a crossing motion over his chest. "I promise," he said.

She threw herself against him and began kissing him. He wanted to ask her why she kept her mouth open, but she wouldn't stop long enough for him to say anything. He unbuttoned her blouse, expecting her to stop him, but she didn't and when he couldn't manage to get her brassiere unfastened, she twisted an arm behind her and did it herself.

"I'm getting hot again," she said.

He didn't know what you were supposed to say when a girl spoke that way to you, so he didn't say anything. He rubbed his hands over her hips and he opened his own mouth to kiss her. He still thought it was a hell of a thing; it made his chin wet, but it did seem to be more fun than just pressing lips.

"Let's lie down," she said.

He flopped down on the ground, panting, and to his amazement she pulled her skirt up to her waist when she lay down beside him. She had no pants on.

She rolled close to him and hung her face into his shoulder while he wiggled out of his own clothes and he thought it was kind of funny that she would be modest.

They made love three times and afterwards Alice said she had never seen anyone as strong as he was.

It never was much harder than that for him. Of course, Alice asked him for a dollar before they got home. He didn't have a dollar and that made her angry, but he didn't care. He never had a girl ask him for a dollar after that, though.

Later he decided his success must be due to the fact that he never asked for anything else. He was just direct and he never treated the ones who said yes any differently than the ones who said no. No girl was ever linked scandalously with him and he never hurt any feelings.

Once, in high school, he wrote a girl a note. It said, "Me Tarzan. You Jane. Bam?" The question mark was very large. That girl laughed about it, but she said no. Most of them said yes.

So in his mind the calendar was cut into the weeks with Nancy, the month with Carla, the days with Polly.

And others.

Jack always thought it was odd, too, that none of the girls seemed to expect more than that from him, either. No one ever pushed him to get married. None ever showed any jealousy.

"But what the hell," he always said, "I never promised them anything more and what I do give is so good they can't bring themselves to complain about anything."

Then he would laugh so hard his huge body would shake.

If he had studied harder he could have stayed in college. But when they flunked him out after three warnings, he didn't care much.

For a while he had thought he wanted to play professional football, but he found that he wasn't fast enough and that his knees weren't strong enough. If he wasn't playing football, he didn't care really about college. They had girls in Massillon, too, so he thought he might as well go back and sell hardware now as later.

Which is what he did until he got drafted and then he met Stone and Leeds. He liked them, especially Burt Stone. Leeds was an oddball. As Stone said in that funny New York accent, "A hipster from Middletown, Ohio?" But Leeds was a man who made you think that he enjoyed being with you but couldn't care less if you went away. He always seemed to be laughing at you.

Stone, though, needed a friend. Jack could sense his loneliness. There was something bothering him, too, Jack could tell. Like they used to do at school. A bunch of guys would sit around and analyze each other.

Sometimes it got pretty rough and once he wanted to smack a guy who said his tomcatting was due to latent homosexuality, but he just laughed that off, too, and found out later the guy was queer himself and had this thing about trying to make everyone else look gay.

16

But if there was something bothering him, Burt didn't want to talk about it so Jack didn't pressure him.

Still Burt's casual cynicism had an attraction for him. That was why he was in on the robbery with them. He didn't understand why Stone was so insistent that he had to get ten thousand dollars, but if Stone needed ten thousand dollars he was willing to help him get it.

Besides, it sounded exciting.

He remembered the night they first thought about it. They had been drinking, the three of them, and Stone was angry because some rich man had just spent two hundred thousand dollars on a party for his daughter.

He was really bitter about it.

"Take it easy," Jack said. "We can't all be rich."

"It's just a damn shame we can't all start off with about ten thousand dollars," Al Leeds said. "Ten thousand would fix me up in a nice garage and start me off right."

Jack and Leeds laughed about it. Stone didn't even appear to be listening to them, but suddenly he leaned across the table and said, "Why the hell don't we just get ourselves a stake?"

Jack and Leeds thought he was kidding, but he wasn't. Leeds was for it immediately. Jack thought about it for a while before he agreed to go in with them. Anyone can use money and this looked like an easy way to get it. Leeds remembered this department store where his fraternity brother had worked and they decided on that for a target. They considered a bank, but bank robbers get chased by federal men and Stone said it wasn't necessary to take on the FBI just to get a stake to start life with.

Even now Jack didn't know for sure exactly why he stayed with them. He didn't need the money. But Stone did. So Jack would help him get it.

And being honest with himself, he admitted that he liked the idea, too. He had never been able to stand inaction. There was always time later to enter his father's business, to join the Kiwanis Club, to marry, to get out of condition.

He considered the possibility that they might get caught, but he dismissed that. There was nothing that would make

17

anyone suspect them. And the way Stone was planning it, nothing unexpected could happen . . .

"I think that's all the information I need then, sir," Jack Cannon said. "I should be able to draw up a very good insurance plan for you."

"All right," the man said. "Say, you look as if you might have played football."

"Guard for three years with the University of Pittsburgh."

"How do you think the Panthers will do this fall?"

Jack grinned and sat back down. "Now you've hit on my favorite subject," he said.

It helped sell the insurance to make small talk, but he thought Al Leeds would have snorted at him calling football his favorite subject.

CHAPTER 3

The motor didn't sound right.

No one but an expert could have heard the faint chugging in the motorcycle's engine, but Alan Leeds heard it. He was kneeling beside the bike, turning the throttle and listening. He was frowning.

He let the motor slow to idling speed and bent his head to listen again. Then with a screwdriver he made an adjustment. When he turned the throttle open again, the chunking was gone from the answering roar and he nodded, smiling.

He turned off the ignition and began to polish the motocycle's painted surfaces. From inside the trailer, he could hear Jack Cannon singing along with a rock and roll star on the radio.

Leeds dropped the rag to the ground and rubbed his hair that he kept in a GI cut. He was twenty-five, but he was satisfied that he looked older. He had never wanted to look like a boy. His hair was black and his skin was olive, but his eyes were a surprising light green. His face was planed sharply; his cheekbones were wide and he looked as if he

18

could be part Indian. On occasion he had claimed to be part Cherokee, but he didn't know whether he really was. His father had been a plant laborer who had no idea who his great-grandfather had been.

The only thing that kept Leeds from being strikingly handsome was that there was no compensating softness about him. He looked as if he ought to carry a gun and talk out of the side of his mouth.

A girl came out of the cement block building that served the trailer park as a communal laundry. She was wearing a pair of black tights and a cotton blouse that was twisted and tied under her breasts. She was carrying a canvas sack of newly-washed laundry. Leeds stood, slouching, and watched her come toward him. She was too slender to bounce like that naturally, so he knew she was watching him, too, and walking that way because she was conscious of his stare.

When she got closer to him, she stumbled slightly over one of the ridges in the street and Leeds laughed and said, "Hey, look at you."

She turned to look directly at him. "That's what you're doing."

"Don't you like it?"

She smiled then. "I don't mind."

He was mildly surprised that she had answered him, but he grinned back and said, "I don't mind what I see, either."

She put down the laundry and walked closer. "Your motorcycle?"

"Mine. I jarred something loose on this street."

"I don't know anything about motorcycles. I thought only juvenile delinquents ride them."

He laughed aloud. "And people who live in trailer parks."

"With that face you could be a delinquent, too."

"What's wrong with my face?"

"Nothing. I'm studying art. Your face would make a beautiful portrait."

"Naturally."

She laughed. "Are you as hard as you look?"

"Harder."

"I'll bet you are."

19

He would have bet she was wearing the tights deliberately. Some women dress immodestly because they don't think of it. Not this one.

"What's your name?"

"Sally Talent," she said crisply.

"Sally Talent, have you any talent?"

"That's not very original."

"I'm not very poetic," Al admitted.

"You live here?"

He jerked a thumb at the trailer. "There."

"I live down there." She pointed to a red Mohawk.

Al knew he was making an impression. He told her his name and they talked.

He half-sat on the seat of the motorcycle and watched her. When she reached into her blouse pocket for a cigarette, he offered her one of his. He lit it for her and she touched his hand to steady the match. He had good hands; he knew women liked them. He never had grease under his fingernails and his hands were smooth and strong. His arms had no hair on them and the muscle in them was corded.

The girl's hair was blonde, hanging loose down her back. She wore no makeup. She was slender, more so than he usually liked, but her breasts were full and her legs looked as if they would be firm. Besides, she looked as if she belonged in a trailer park . . .

Al Leeds was tough. He had been all his life. The older he got the more he realized that he wasn't stupid either. He learned that he liked to read. But any intellectualism in his life he kept to himself. The face he showed was a fighter's face. He had a scar on his cheek and he was proud of it. He thought it illustrated his personality.

In a way, it did.

His mother loved him when he was a boy. No one else ever did that he knew of. He and his father got along well enough; they just let each other alone. Leeds sometimes suspected that his father rather liked having a hood for a son. And Leeds didn't kid himself. He was a hood.

Not that he was ever in trouble with the law. He never

stole anything. But being a hood is a state of mind, not the result of actions, and he always had that attitude.

He never knew why either. All he knew for sure was that Al Leeds was tough.

Girls came easy to Al. He learned early that girls always come easy to hoods. He assumed always that they knew the score. He never lied to one because he never told any girl he loved her.

He only had one scruple. He was never able to explain to himself why he had that one, but he did. And a girl named Ruth broke it. She was the daughter of a professor in the Ohio State English department.

"Why didn't you tell me?" he said that night.

She was crying. "I was afraid you wouldn't then."

"You should have told me I was the first."

"But you said you'd leave if I kept on shoving you away."

He remembered feeling frustrated. "That's right," he said. "But why the hell didn't you tell me?"

"Oh Alan," she said. She tried to put her arms around him, but he pushed her aside and walked out of the house without looking back.

Later that night, at the fraternity house, a pledge woke him and told him he was wanted on the telephone.

"Al," she said when he answered. "Al, you've got to come back here."

"Forget it," he said.

"You have to."

"I don't have to do anything."

"Al, I love you."

"Nobody loves nobody but Jesus and he's left town." He forced a harshness that he did not feel. He felt uncomfortable, sorry for the girl, but he felt as if she had betrayed him somehow and he didn't want to see her or to talk to her ever again.

When all she did was cry, he hung up.

A few days later the dean of men called him in. He had Al sent into the office and before Al even sat down he said, "You're in trouble, young man."

"What kind of trouble?"

"I think you know what kind of trouble."

Al kept his voice and his face impassive. "My grades are okay. I haven't done any cheating and I haven't stolen anything. What kind of trouble can I be in?"

"It's about Ruth Champion."

"What about her?"

"Her father is very upset."

"I don't know what you're talking about."

"Young man, I have no intention of playing cat and mouse with you."

"Then come to the point."

The dean leaned forward. "Listen," he said. "I don't like your kind. And I'm telling you in language you can understand. You had better leave school. Today."

"Go to hell."

"If you stay, I guarantee you that you will fail every course you are taking. Professor Champion is well-liked and respected here. If you stay, you'll think you are already in hell."

Leeds looked at the dean for a few seconds, then stood up and walked out without answering. He knew the dean meant what he said.

It rankled to be thrown out, but aside from that he didn't care much. He had only come to college in the first place because it was a change from Middletown and because he didn't know what else to do with himself.

During the next three years he worked at various jobs and he hung around the stock track near Cleveland until someone let him drive in a race. He won and he drove regularly after that. Most of the other drivers didn't like to drive against him, but they liked to watch him. He drove recklessly. He hit curves too fast just because it was fun to feel the rear end whip around. He crashed twice and walked away both times.

Sometimes when he passed other drivers they would think they heard him laughing out loud.

When his draft notice came, he didn't want to go. Someone told him that if he would eat soap the night before his physical, the x-ray would show spots on his lungs. He ate soap until he vomited, but the x-ray showed him in excellent physical condition. When he left three days later for basic training, he could still taste the soap.

He was a good soldier. He liked the army and that surprised him. He did what he was told and he generally did it better than anyone else. He was tough, but so were the sergeants who trained him and he found that he respected them. So he set out to make them respect him, too.

He was a sergeant himself when they discharged him. Although he hadn't told Cannon and Stone, he was planning on re-enlisting when they had finished with the department store robbery. At first he thought he would buy a garage because he liked cars. But now that he was out he missed the army. When he was in, he felt as if he belonged to something.

First, though, he did want a share of that department store money.

He was surprised that Stone and Cannon were in on this. They didn't strike him as the type. For him the world only had one law: if you want it, take it. But they didn't think that way. Cannon was just a big, good-natured cluck and Stone had something on his mind half the time.

Al wasn't sure either that he could trust Stone—but if anyone was going to make off with the whole pile, it was going to be Al Leeds. He didn't intend to doublecross the others, but he sure as hell didn't intend to let them doublecross him.

One thing was sure, though. He wasn't going to spend the rest of his life selling television sets to middle-aged jerks who had worn themselves out and didn't have anything better to do than watch television at night.

He went along with it when Stone suggested that kind of job. He still went out to the stock car track on the west side of town on Saturdays and pretty soon now he was going to convince some car owner to let him drive. If Stone thought working in that appliance store gave them a better front, he'd do it. It wasn't going to be much longer.

And he didn't really mind selling television sets. Women were particularly easy for him to sell. They would look at him when they came in with their husbands and he could

23

always tell which ones were wishing they could feel hard muscle again instead of the slack guts they had to sleep with.

He got some laughs from that.

Still, he'd be glad when Stone was ready to go . . .

Sally Talent said, "How long have you been in Columbus?"

"Too long if I'm just now meeting you."

"Come on, hard guy," she said. "That's not your kind of speech." But she was pleased.

"Why don't you invite me down for a cup of coffee."

"My roommate is there."

"Sometime when she's not there?"

"I'd love it."

"That sounds like an invitation."

"It'll be whatever you can make of it," she said archly, blowing smoke in his face.

He grinned. "How many roommates?"

"Two. But one of them is working now."

"I live with a couple of guys. Your girls would like them. How about a little party-type thing Saturday night."

"All right," she agreed.

"Don't you have to ask your friends?"

"Social life around here is nil. And not many guys ask us out just for a date. They figure trailer-park girls are easy marks. All you have to do is mention that you live in a trailer park and right away everyone figures you're fifteen minutes out of the mountains and ripe for a city boy to educate."

Al laughed with her. "You'll come then?"

"We'll come." She picked up her laundry. "I have to go."

"About nine o'clock Saturday."

"Great." She patted his cheek. "Take care of your motorcycle, hard guy."

"Hey," he called when she had gone a few steps. "Come naked Saturday. It'll save time."

She grinned back at him. "I'm not in any hurry," she said.

24

He watched her walk away. Stone wasn't going to like this party bit, he knew, but to hell with Stone. It had been a long time.

CHAPTER 4

"Wait till you see who I just met," Sally Talent said as she entered the Mohawk trailer. It was smaller than the one shared by Leeds and the two others, but there was more open space in it and it looked roomier.

Fran Novak came out of the larger bedroom. She was short, with curly brown hair, and her figure was full. She had a wide, pleasant looking face, and if she wasn't particularly pretty, she was attractive and warm-looking. "Who?" she said.

"I met one of those men who live in that silver trailer down the street. And he invited us all down for a party Saturday night."

"Just like that," Fran said.

"Sure," Sally said, "it'll be fun." She dropped flat on the couch and kicked her legs up in the air. "It's been so long since I've had any excitement, I've been wishing old man Gardner up at the gate house would try to rape me or something."

"I'd think you were kidding if I didn't know you so well," Fran said, laughing.

"Well, don't you ever get bored?"

"Not so bored that Mr. Gardner gets to me."

"This town is enough to drive me nuts." Sally sat up. "But this man I just met sure isn't the dull type. He looks like Marlon Brando and he has muscles like Burt Lancaster."

"There's more to life than muscles and excitement."

"Not for me. And someday soon I'm going to pack up and leave this town."

"You'll settle down more when you get older."

"Some people are born settled," Sally said. "You for

instance. You'll probably be happier in your life than I will in mine, but I'll have more excitement."

Fran looked at her seriously. "I wouldn't doubt it," she said . . .

Sally Talent knew something of the difference between happiness and excitement. At least, she knew what excitement was. Happiness, she thought, would be a quiet contentment and she could imagine what it was even if she had never felt it. She thought Fran was happy that way and she told herself that she envied Fran, but she knew that more truthfully she felt a contempt for Fran. She hid it, but it was real.

Fran was older and sometimes she was condescending because of it, but Sally knew Fran was really pretty innocent. She was grown up and she had matured sexually and all that, but she just wasn't sharp. To Sally it was right to do what you wanted to do and wrong to do something you didn't. She knew Fran didn't feel that way.

But then she also knew Fran didn't know everything she did about the world.

At twenty years of age, Sally was a junior at Ohio State University. That is, she had been attending the school for three years. But she hadn't completed the required amount of work for junior standing and her grades were just good enough to keep her from flunking out.

She told people she was an artist, but she knew she didn't have the talent to be serious about it and she didn't care.

Because it didn't matter. She didn't want to be an artist. She didn't want to be anything. What she was sure of was that she didn't want to be ordinary, to get married and raise children in a suburb. It frightened her to think that might happen to her.

She believed in love, but not in marriage. Marriage was her mother and father. Love was a naked woman, sitting up in bed, her hair around her shoulders.

She wasn't bitter about it—or at least she didn't think she was bitter about it any more. But the two images, love and marriage, didn't mix well in her mind.

26

That started when she was ten years old and her father was away on business overnight. Sally was asleep, but something woke her, some noise, and she lay for a while trying to figure out what it was. She heard noise coming from her mother's bedroom.

She thought her father had come home and she got out of bed to go see him. She padded out through the hall and went into the other bedroom.

It was dark and she couldn't see well, but there was a naked man lying on his stomach beside her mother with his head on her breasts. Sally thought it was her father and she spoke to him.

Her mother said, "My God," and sat up in bed. She was naked, too, and her hair was loose instead of in curlers the way it usually was when she was in bed. "Sally, go to bed," she said.

"I want to see Daddy."

"Daddy's tired."

"I just want to kiss him."

She started toward the bed, but her mother got up quickly and took her by the shoulder and made her go back to her own bedroom.

Sally didn't understand why she couldn't kiss her father, but she went back to sleep.

When she woke in the morning the man was gone. Sally asked her mother about him, but her mother said she must have been dreaming. Sally was sure she hadn't been, but her mother became angry so she didn't say anything more about it.

Her father came home late that evening. Sally never knew who the man was she saw in bed with her mother.

About a year after that she found out what it was her mother and the man had been doing. Then she hated her mother for a long time.

But when she was about fourteen, she overheard her parents. They were arguing and she heard her mother say, "Don't talk to me about what you're going to do. I told you the truth because you asked me and I don't care if you do know. I know what you do and most of the time I even know who you do it with."

Her father said, "You don't have proof of anything."

"Are you going to tell me it's not true?"

"I'm not telling you anything."

"Well don't."

"It's different with a man."

"Listen," her mother said, "I don't care how many women you sleep with. I made up my mind to that long ago. I can get all the men I want and I want a lot of them."

There was more, but she didn't listen. She was afraid someone at school would find out about her mother and father, but she didn't hate her mother any more. She didn't hate her father either. She just didn't know how to act around them. She didn't want them to know that she knew.

Sometimes it puzzled her that they didn't divorce each other, but then she would think that they didn't have to do that. They didn't fight much; both of them had the freedom to do what they pleased, and they had a reasonably comfortable home. Probably, she thought, other homes weren't any happier.

Only she thought about it a lot and she took her first lover when she was fifteen. He was sixteen and he was clumsy, but she wasn't sorry. It was an easy thing for her and she didn't care when the boy talked about it. It was fun and it was exciting and she enjoyed the way boys looked at her.

But she got into trouble once and that's when she told her mother and father that she knew about the way they lived.

She was sixteen and she had been invited to a party that was being held at a cabin near a small lake just outside town. She had expected there would be a chaperone but when she arrived, no adults were present.

One of the boys brought a case of beer and they drank it warm because there was no refrigerator at the cabin. They danced and some of the couples paired off and went outside where it was dark, but nothing much happened until just after midnight when someone suggested they go swimming.

One of the girls said, "We don't have any bathing suits here."

"That's the idea," someone said.

It had been meant as a joke, but no one wanted to be the one to back out, so they all went down to the beach area. When they got there, though, one of the girls stopped and said, "I'm not going to do this."

Sally said, "Why not? Are you ashamed of the way you look?"

"You show her how it's done, Sally," said one of the boys.

Everyone was quiet and watching her. She had already unbuttoned her blouse and she finished undressing slowly, taking her time. When she was naked, she straightened up and said, "I'm ready."

One of the other girls began to undress.

After that everyone undressed, even the girl who had said she wouldn't. They ran into the water, yelling and laughing, but for a while the girls and boys stayed apart. Then one of the boys swam over under water and grabbed Sally's legs and pulled her under the surface. The other boys followed him.

Sally swam away, but the boy followed her until he caught up with her. They were in deep water and they had to tread water while they looked at each other.

Sally said, "What do you want?"

"You."

"What are you going to do with me after you get me?"

"I'll show you if you want me to."

They were apart from the others and the coldness of the water made her shiver. "You'll have to catch me," she said. She twisted and began swimming for the shore.

The boy caught her about halfway in. She jerked when he grabbed her. Without thinking, she thrust out with her legs and they went around his waist.

They began to sink. He let go and tried to push her away, but she put her arms around him and held on until he had to put his hand under her chin and force her head back. Then she let go and he swam to the top. When she

29

came up, he was looking for her and he was frightened. "What are you trying to do?" he said.

"You wanted it."

"I didn't want to drown."

"Let's go ashore," she said.

He didn't answer her. He just turned and swam toward the beach. She followed him.

Afterwards, she remembered that she felt proud of herself just then. It was crazy, but she hadn't intended to let go of him. She had wanted to hold on to him, her legs around his waist, until they sank down to the bottom. She didn't want to die, but she wanted to just float in that water forever.

She remembered, too, that she didn't feel the boy was leading her to the beach. She was driving him.

He was a big, loose-muscled boy, and when he stood up on the beach and looked back for her, she thought he was beautiful. She wanted him worse than she had ever wanted anyone, but she hated him, too, and she was anxious to get with him because she wanted to punish him for letting her go out there in the water.

They went behind a large rock and when they lay down, it was she who pushed him back flat in the sand and it was she who made love to him.

It was a strange, wild way she felt and later she thought that she might have been insane that night. She wanted the act of love to hurt him because she wanted to punish him and yet she wanted it to be so great that he would never forget it no matter how many women he slept with in his life.

She never forgot the way she felt that night. In college she took a course in psychology and it made her think she might really have been trying to punish her mother and father for the lovers each of them had had. Maybe she was trying to hurt her father and outdo her mother. She didn't know. But she knew there was something because she didn't try to hide or get away when the police came.

The two policemen were enjoying themselves. Someone from around the curve of the lake had complained because of the noise and the two men had come out, but they hadn't expected to find what they did. They didn't make much effort to keep people from getting away, but they kept their lights bright on the beach and they laughed so hard they were hoarse.

They were taking down names when Sally walked into the circle of light. She looked at them for an instant and then began slowly picking up her clothes.

"Hey," one of the policemen said, "where have you been?"

"Out behind a rock getting laid," she said, looking up. "Don't you feel sorry for yourself that you were too late to get in on the fun?"

She never knew why she reacted that way. She could have cried and pretended to be embarrassed and maybe she could have talked her way out of it, but after the way she talked, the cops had to decide that she was probably the ringleader. One of the girls was glad to help them; she told them Sally was the first one to take off her clothes.

They were charged with delinquency but all of them except Sally were let off with reprimands. She was put on probation for twelve months and warned that a second offense would get her sent to a reformatory.

The wild feeling had disappeared and Sally was embarrassed now about what had happened. She didn't feel any guilt or shame, but she was sorry that everyone knew about it. She didn't show it, though. She was defiant and she wouldn't say she was sorry.

After they left the court the day of her appearance, her parents took her home. They made her sit in the living room and they sat down across from her. "What do you think we should do, Sally?" her father said. "We trusted you and you let us down."

She didn't say anything. For the first time she wanted to cry, but she stared at them, dry-eyed, and wouldn't answer.

"We've tried to give you a good home," her mother said.

They talked to her, one after the other, until their voices ran together and she couldn't understand what they were saying.

Finally they stopped and her father said, "Well, say something, for God's sake."

"Go screw yourselves," she whispered. Her throat felt closed. She wanted to speak in a normal voice, but all she could do was whisper. "You've done it with everyone else in town."

Her father started up from his chair as if he were going to come after her, but he stopped and sat back down again. Sally waited, but neither of them said anything so she rose and walked past them into her bedroom.

Neither she nor they ever mentioned the party or her probation again.

When she graduated from high school, her father insisted she go to college. She did; it would have been too much trouble to fight it.

But she had changed. The wild wanton feeling came more often and she couldn't do without noise and excitement. She didn't bother much with men simply because she didn't find many who excited her. She just wanted crowds and music and lights.

But Al Leeds excited her . . .

"You'll go to the party, won't you?" she said to Fran.

"Sure. Why not?" She laughed. "I'm not exactly an old lady yet, child."

"But you're such a quiet type."

"Only compared to you."

"Do you think Marianne will go?"

"I don't know. You know how she is. You'll have to ask her when she gets home from the hospital."

CHAPTER 5

When the patient had been finished and wheeled into the recovery room, Marianne Nirvell began to relax. She stepped out into the hall and had to consciously keep her shoulders from slumping with exhaustion.

She wanted a cigarette. The doctor who had operated was

in the lounge. "Hi," he said. "Patient all tucked away?"

"She's in recovery." She sat down and took the cigarette the doctor offered.

"In a month's time she'll be as good as new."

Marianne lit her cigarette and rested her head on the back of the couch. "I'm tired tonight," she said.

"When are you due to go off?"

"Two hours ago."

"Why didn't you go home?" he queried, his eyes gently regarding her.

"Because we had to operate."

"Someone else could have assisted."

"I wanted to."

"Well, you're a good nurse," the doctor said.

"Thank you, sir."

"Think nothing of it. I'm just leading up to a seduction."

Marianne smiled. The doctor was sixty years old and proud of his grandchildren.

He stood up now and stretched. "I'm going home," he said. "And so should you."

"I am. Just as soon as I finish this cigarette."

The streets outside the hospital were quiet. Across the way she could see the lights of the university library.

The patient upstairs was someone else's responsibility now, and the operation had only been an appendectomy, but Marianne couldn't help thinking of her. The woman was young and unmarried and some day a husband would uncover what should be perfect skin and he would find a scar.

It made her want to cry.

Marianne Nirvell was a good nurse. She worked hard and she knew her business. She avoided the word, even in her own thinking, because it sounded pretentious, but she was a dedicated nurse. Her parents hadn't wanted her to be one at all. Her father had said he didn't want his daughter carrying bedpans. And he said he'd be damned if he'd pay for her education if she went ahead and enrolled in nurse's training despite his objections.

But she did enroll and he did pay for her education and no one was prouder than he when she led her class. He said, "By God, that girl has a mind of her own and she'll be the best damn nurse that was ever in a hospital."

But he didn't know the whole story. Only three people did.

For the first few years of her life, Marianne Nirvell was just another little girl. She did well in school, but she did nothing that was especially outstanding.

But she was extraordinarily beautiful.

Marianne's mother and father loved her very much and because she was their only child, they were afraid they would spoil her. So they told her she was pretty; she could see that by looking in the mirror, but they never told her she was beautiful.

And she didn't know that she was.

She grew into a tall, gracefully slender woman. Her skin was very fair and her hair was a deep auburn brown and she wore it long because it was naturally curly. Her eyes were dark blue, nearly black, and her face was planed sharply so that it gave her a classic look. She thought her mouth was too large, but it wasn't, and she hardly needed lipstick to give it color.

Sometimes her mother and father wondered how they had come to give birth to such a beautiful thing.

At first, Marianne thought she must be ugly. She was hardly ever asked for a date, but by the time she was sixteen she had learned that she was beautiful. She frightened the high school boys. She would have liked to date them, but they never asked her. They were afraid she would laugh at them or humiliate them and so they went out with the girls who were only cute and they stayed away from Marianne.

So she began to date boys who were older.

And then when she was not quite seventeen, she fell in love.

His name was Tom Herbert and he was twenty-one years old and a junior at the University of Michigan. He was planning to be a lawyer and he wanted to go into politics.

Marianne met him during the spring of her junior year in high school. She was at a country club dance and it seemed to her that Tom must be the one meant for her.

34

He was struck by her beauty, but he wasn't afraid of her, and he talked to her as if he assumed that she was as intelligent as she was beautiful. He was poised and confident and he was handsome. He was nearly six feet tall and his hair was blond and crew-cut and he had a nice smile.

They went together all that summer and they talked of being married. Tom didn't press her to sleep with him, but she knew he wanted her so one August night they made love on a blanket near the shore of a lake.

She was surprised at how wonderful it was. All the way home she was quiet because she was thinking of the way her skin felt, of the way her breasts tingled, and the way the warmth climbed in her groin until she had had to cry out.

When her parents came home that night from their bridge party, she was asleep, naked on her bed, and her mother covered her with a sheet and let her sleep.

Marianne and Tom made love often that summer. She didn't feel guilty about it. She loved him and she was sure he loved her. They would be married some day and they would always have this early part of their love to look back on.

In early September, Marianne became pregnant. She didn't go to a doctor, but she knew. She was sorry that it had happened so soon, but she wasn't unhappy.

She told Tom about it as soon as she was sure. They had been to a movie and they were at a drive-in restaurant. She put her head on his shoulder and told him that she was going to have his baby.

He didn't move at first and then, without looking at her, he said, "Are you sure?"

"Yes."

"When?"

"In about seven months."

"You're sure you're pregnant?"

His voice sounded odd and she raised up to look at him. His face was pale and his lips were trembling. "I'm sure," she said.

"What are we going to do?"

35

She had thought they would go somewhere and be married, but she couldn't say that to him. "I don't know," she said quietly. "What do you think we ought to do?"

"I don't know," he said. "My God!"

She began to cry.

"I'll have to quit school," he said. "I don't know what I'll do."

"Take me home," she said. "Please."

She didn't hear anything from him for two weeks. She was scared and ashamed, but she didn't say anything to anyone. She didn't even tell her mother although she knew that her parents would be understanding and helpful. But she didn't want anyone to know. It wasn't her pregnancy of which she was ashamed. She didn't want to have to tell anyone that the father of her unborn child didn't want her after all.

After two weeks, Tom called her and said he would pick her up that evening. He didn't say anything else and neither did she. When he arrived, she was waiting.

He took her to a dirty brick apartment building and she looked at it and said, "What are we going to do here?"

"There's a doctor here."

"I told you I'm sure I'm pregnant."

"Let's go see him anyway."

She didn't want to go; she was scared, but she let him lead her up three flights of stairs. He knocked on a door and a man opened it.

"What do you want?" he said.

Tom said, "We're looking for Doctor Adams."

"Are you Tom Herbert?"

"Yes."

The man opened the door further. Tom pushed Marianne into the apartment ahead of him.

"Take her into that other room," the man said. "Get her clothes off her and have her lie down on the table."

"Tom," Marianne said.

He held her by the arm and took her into a smaller room. There was a white cabinet in it and a flat, padded table, but nothing else.

"Listen," Tom said, whispering. "This is the only thing we can do."

"What's he going to do?" she whispered nervously.

"He's going to get rid of the baby."

"No." She tried to pull away, but he held on tighter.

"Do you want to ruin both our lives?" Tom said. "This way we'll both be out of it."

"No," she said. "I won't do it."

He slapped her across the face.

She touched her cheek with one hand, but she didn't say anything. She looked at him and she thought he was going to cry. "My dad gave me the money for this," he said. "It's costing three hundred dollars."

"Get out of here," she said, suddenly feeling cold and numb and miserable. "I have to take off my clothes."

Marianne wouldn't open her eyes when the doctor came into the room and she shook all over when he examined her, but he was surprisingly gentle and didn't talk much. The operation didn't take as long as she had thought it would, but it hurt so much that he had to give her a wad of tape to bite on to keep from yelling.

She was sick for a week afterwards and she was frightentd by the pain she felt. She knew she should be in a hospital but she couldn't do that so she just endured it.

She never spoke to Tom Herbert after that night. Occasionally she saw him on the street, but she wouldn't look at him. Once he tried to call her, but she wouldn't go to the phone. Her mother was curious about that, but she didn't pry. Marianne just said that she and Tom had had a fight and her mother didn't ask her any more.

The pain left her body eventually, but it never left her mind. They had scraped a baby from her womb, and it tortured her that she had allowed it to be done.

She cried easily and she tried to write some poetry, but she realized that she was overdramatizing herself and trying to rationalize herself into a tragic heroine when what she really was was the guilty culprit of a sordid situation.

That's why she had decided to become a nurse. She

couldn't escape the guilt of what she had done, but she could assuage it by helping others.

At least, that's what she thought. And it did help her. She was intelligent enough to know that she was engaging in personal therapy, but she was also intelligent enough to realize that she had to go on living and that what she did at seventeen didn't necessarily have to affect her whole life.

Sometimes she still felt as if she were the only woman in history with a tragic past, but she was learning to laugh at herself, and she was learning to live with herself.

She took another lover during her second year of training, but it was rather like the trapeze artist who goes back up immediately after falling. The man didn't last long, but he finished cleaning Tom Herbert out of her system.

In any event she became an excellent nurse and that made her feel that she had a purpose in life. So she didn't have many nights when she lay awake, thinking of the baby she didn't have . . .

"You've been working too hard," Sally Talent said to her with a quizzical look on her face. "You need some relaxation."

"I already said I'd go to your party."

"But you don't look very enthusiastic."

"That's because she hasn't seen that man of yours who looks like Marlon Brando," Fran Novak said.

CHAPTER 6

Burt Stone was angry.

He was standing in the middle of the trailer, looking at Al Leeds.

"What the hell were you thinking of?" he demanded harshly, his rugged face ridged with concern.

Leeds didn't answer, but Jack Cannon came in from the kitchen area and said, "I think it sounds like fun."

"I thought we agreed to stay free until after the job was done."

"Jesus Christ," Leeds said suddenly.

"We agreed to it," Stone insisted.

"And we're about to go nuts around here, man."

"All we need is to get tangled up with some women."

"You have something against women?" Leeds asked.

"I like women as well as you do, buddy, but not in an operation like this."

"So all I did was invite the three of them down for Saturday night. How much trouble can that cause us?"

"Plenty," Stone said. He rubbed his face hard and started to turn away, but he spun back and said, "You should have known better."

"Wait till you see what they look like," Leeds said.

"I don't give a good goddamn what they look like."

"Anyone want a beer?" Cannon said trying to ease the tension.

"Get Stone one," Leeds said. "He needs to cool off."

"I don't want to cool off. I want to get out of having this damned party Saturday night."

"What do you want me to do?" Leeds said, his voice rising. "Maybe I should go down there and tell them my father doesn't allow me to have girls in my trailer."

"Jesus Christ," Stone said. "You talk like a moron."

"What the hell's wrong with meeting some women?"

"We talked about it before."

"And you said we'd be a damn sight better off if we didn't make any friends or get involved with any women until after the job was all done. Okay. But one evening with three girls isn't going to make any difference."

"You dumb bastard," Stone said. Leeds started to get up and Stone pointed a finger at him. "You get up off that couch and I'll kick your teeth out."

"I don't think you can," snapped Leeds, his eyes hooded.

"Maybe not, but I'll sure as hell give it a try."

"What are you so hot about?"

"One evening you think. These three dames live just down the street from us. You think we can party with them Saturday night and then they're just going to forget us? If

I know you, you've already got the one picked out that you intend to get into."

"We don't have to tell them anything," Leeds pointed out.

"You'd better not."

"I still think it sounds like fun," Jack Cannon said. "We can play drop the clothespin in the milk bottle and like that."

Stone wheeled to look at him and began to laugh. "Shut up, you cluck," he said. "I'm having enough trouble with Al."

Leeds had started to laugh, too. "You have to admit it's been a long time since we've been around anything softer than Cannon's head."

"I know it," Stone said. "I like women, too."

"What are you complaining about, then?"

"I just don't like the idea of entanglements."

"Then you go down and tell them it's off."

That's what he wanted to do, but he knew he couldn't do that. There wasn't anything he could say that would sound logical. "Forget it," Stone said. "We'll have your party. But watch what you drink and watch your mouth."

"You watch your own mouth. I can take care of myself."

For a second, Stone tensed, wanting to jerk Leeds to his feet, but he turned away. "All right," he said. "You got us into this. Now we have to go through with it."

"I still think it sounds like fun," Jack Cannon said.

"I'm going to throw a goddamn beer can at you if you say that again," Stone said.

"A full one, I hope."

"Oh shut up. I'm going to take a shower."

He went back through the trailer and began to take off his clothes in the bedroom. He could hear Leeds and Cannon in the front, laughing about the three girls who were coming down Saturday. Maybe he shouldn't blame them. It *had* been a long time. The thought of having a woman made him shake. But he knew that they would have been better off if they had stuck to their original agreement.

40

I want that money, he thought. And Leeds had better not mess it up.

He could sense a tension growing between him and Leeds and he wasn't sure of its cause. Sometimes they were like two cats in a movie cartoon, stalking each other, fur bristling. And Cannon was a big, good-natured bull dog who was trying to keep them apart.

Everything has to be right, he thought. It takes patience and Leeds doesn't have any.

He thought about the guns, the three automatics. Leeds had stolen them just before they left the Army and they had two boxes of ammunition for each of the weapons. They had joked about the guns and Cannon said they made him feel like Billy the Kid, but he wondered what would happen if someone tried to get in the way.

Oh for the life of a criminal. For God's sake.

How much is there left to do? I'm getting as restless as Leeds. We have the guns and we have the getaway mapped, but we have to know the exact layout of the store. We'll have to have someone buy something in there. Cannon can do that. He's less likely to be conspicuous than Leeds. And we'll have to watch the store to see whether there are any cops at all who patrol that area.

He finished undressing and went into the shower stall.

The water came down icy and it made him shiver, but it felt good and he turned his face toward the spray and let it cover him.

He thought again about the party. It made him nervous to think of the girls knowing them. As long as no one knew them, no one would comment on anything they did.

But there was nothing he could do about it now.

To hell with it. He began to think about the ten thousand dollars he would have and he could almost see himself in medical school.

Dr. Burton Stone, he mused.

CHAPTER 7

Al Leeds had bought a portable record player and twenty long-playing records. He said a party doesn't begin until the lights go down and the music goes on.

This party had begun. Jack Cannon was talking to Fran Novak in the kitchen. Stone could see them laughing together over the ingredients of a drink they were inventing. Leeds was dancing with Sally Talent. They were hardly moving and her eyes were closed.

Stone said, "They look happy."

Marianne Nirvell put out her cigarette and didn't answer him.

"I'm sorry I brought it up," Stone said.

"I didn't know you expected an answer to a statement like that."

"Forget it."

"All right."

He looked at her and their eyes met for an instant, but both of them glanced away quickly. "Do you like being a nurse?" he said.

"Of course, or I wouldn't be doing it."

To hell with you, Stone said to himself. You may be beautiful, but to hell with you. I don't like you and I don't have to be polite to you. But, out loud, he said, "Would you like to dance?"

"No."

"No thank you."

She looked at him sharply, but she didn't smile. "Just no," she said.

"All right," he said. He wanted to get away from her. "I'm going to get a drink."

He was halfway to the kitchen when she said, "Bring me one please." He glanced back, surprised because she had refused a drink earlier, and she was smiling. He walked back to her. "What would you like?" he said.

"I think a gin and tonic."

He wanted to say something, but he couldn't think of anything that wouldn't be stupid. He wanted to say: I think you're the most beautiful human being I have ever seen. And he wanted to say: I hate you, Marianne Nirvell. You're beautiful, but you're trouble for me and you act as if you're doing me a favor just to talk to me. And if I get close to you, I'm a damn fool.

"I'll get your drink," he said.

Cannon and Fran Novak were still in the kitchen. She was leaning against the refrigerator and Cannon was standing over her, one big arm on either side of her so she couldn't get away. They were laughing and Cannon was saying, "I do too think a woman should be plump."

"Where the hell's the gin?" Stone said.

"Ask the butler," Cannon said and Fran laughed at him.

Stone turned to look at Marianne. She was staring at him and she didn't look away, but her face was expressionless.

He wanted to shout at her. He wanted to step out and look her right in the face and say, "What the hell are you looking at?"

But he made the drinks and took them back to the couch. He handed her one of the glasses before he sat down.

"Thank you," she said.

"You're welcome."

She began to laugh softly. "We're a lot more formal than they are, aren't we?" She nodded at Leeds and Sally. They were still dancing.

"I don't believe in being familiar with women who don't like me," Stone said. Then he wondered why he had said that. He had never been so attracted to a woman, but he resented her. Her beauty? The fact that he knew he shouldn't get involved? Her apparent dislike for him? He didn't know and what difference did it make anyway?

"I didn't say I don't like you," Marianne said.

"But I'm hardly your ideal."

"You could be more pleasant."

"So could you."

43

To hell with it, he thought. Just goddamn it to hell with it anyway.

"What do you do?" she said.

"I'm a bartender."

"You don't have to be belligerent about it."

"I'm not."

"I don't care if you're a spaceman."

"That's obvious."

Marianne smiled suddenly. "I sound like a first class bitch, don't I?"

"Yes."

"And you sound like a confirmed woman-hater."

"Do I?"

The music stopped and they looked up. "Hey," Stone said. "You two can stop dancing. There's no more music."

Sally said, "Put more on, Al." She was flushed.

Leeds went to the record player to restack the records. Sally went with him and as she waited, she put her arm around his waist.

"Ah, God," Marianne whispered.

"What's the matter?"

"Nothing."

"Is it them?"

"No. Not really."

"They should make a good pair."

"All right," she said. "Don't talk about it."

He felt a rising resentment again, but he wanted to kiss her so badly he couldn't look at her mouth and his throat was dry.

"Let's get out of here," he said.

"What?"

"Let's go for a ride."

"You've been drinking."

"Not much."

She looked down at the floor and closed her eyes. He started to tell her to forget it, but she said, "All right, let's go."

He stood up and walked over to Cannon. "Give me your car keys," he said.

"You're running out on us?"

"I'm going for a drive."

"Alone?"

"No, not alone, damn it. Give me the keys."

Fran laughed and said, "He sounds dangerous."

Cannon had stopped smiling and he was looking at Stone closely. "Are you all right?" he said.

"Give me the keys."

"Okay. Just take it easy."

Marianne was waiting at the door. Stone took her arm and opened the screen door. Leeds called, "Where do you think you're going?"

Stone took Marianne out the door without answering. He heard Leeds say, "What the hell's the matter with him?" And he heard Sally Talent laugh harshly.

He drove straight out Westerville Road, out of Columbus. Marianne sat against the door, as far from him as possible, and they didn't speak until he was through Westerville and on the open highway.

Then Marianne said, "Slow down."

"I'm not drunk."

"I know you're not, but you're driving seventy miles an hour."

"Sorry," he said. "I didn't aim to scare you."

"I'm not scared."

He stared ahead of him and he said, "Damn you anyway."

"Why?"

"I don't know why."

"Do you dislike me so much?"

He laughed. "No," he said. "I don't dislike you at all."

He swung the car hard and spun onto a side road. The turn threw her across the seat and she fell against him. She straightened, but she stayed close to him. She was trembling.

"I'm sorry," he said.

"Sorry for what?"

"Sorry, just sorry, goddamn it." His voice trailed off. He stopped the car and turned off the lights.

"What do you want?" she said.

"Nothing."

"Why did you stop?"

"Listen," he said, ignoring her question. "I think you're the most beautiful woman I've ever seen."

"Thank you."

"Don't thank me."

"All right. I take it back."

"I think you're beautiful, but I don't want you."

"What?" She looked at him, her eyes startled and wary.

"I don't want you."

"I don't want you either."

"Good."

He stared out through the windshield.

"Are we going to sit here all night?" she said.

"I don't know. Maybe."

"Burt."

"What?"

"Nothing."

He turned his head to look at her. "Do you want me to take you home?"

"When you're ready," she said gently, no inflection in her voice.

"That's not what I asked you."

"There's nothing at home that I'm in a hurry to get back to. I can wait for a while."

"Do you want a cigarette?"

"Yes."

He lit them and she watched his face. When he handed her the cigarette, she brushed his hand. "You know," she said. "I'm trying to hate you."

"Why?"

She hesitated and he took a deep pull on his cigarette and held the smoke in his lungs. "I'm not sure why," she said finally.

"Is it working? Do you hate me?"

"No."

"I don't hate you, either," he murmured, feeling an ache deep inside him.

"But you don't want me?"

"I'm trying not to."

"Is it working?" she whispered, her voice dry and taut.

"No."

He switched on the ignition and started the car.

"Where are we going now?" she said.

"Just riding."

"All right." She put her head back on the seat.

"Is it all right?"

"Yes. Let's ride."

He drove slowly back to the main highway and then turned north again, away from Columbus. She didn't speak to him or look at him and he wondered if she had gone to sleep.

He knew he had never wanted a woman as badly as he wanted this one, but he knew that he had better not want her. She was beautiful, but she was sharp. There was an edge to her, and he wanted to dislike her for it. All evening he had twisted between wanting to kiss her and wanting to hit her.

She could see him without turning her head and she kept her eyes nearly closed because she didn't want him to know she was watching him. It frightened her, the way she felt about him, and she thought that she should probably be just a little afraid of him, too. There was a look about his eyes, something cold or lost, and it repelled her, but it caught her and fascinated her, too.

Back there, when the car was stopped, she had been afraid that he would try to grab her, but he hadn't and for some queer, perverse reason, that made her want him.

A perfect stranger, she thought. What kind of slut gets hot for a perfect stranger?

She used harsh words; she wanted to feel revulsion. But she didn't. And she knew that she wouldn't resist anything he did if he stopped the car again. She hated herself for it; she knew she should protect herself. But she knew that she wouldn't be able to do anything about it.

She didn't want to want him. She wanted to hate him, to get away from him.

No.

What she really wanted was to ride in darkness and silence and to look at him, at the way his skin seemed so white because his hair was so black. And his mouth was thin and wide-slashed and it looked as if it would be hard enough to hurt her.

"It's getting late," he said, after a long interval of silence.
"Yes."
"Maybe we'd better get back."
"I suppose so. How far have we come?"
"I don't know. Fifty miles, sixty maybe."
He slowed, made a U turn, and started back toward the city.
"Marianne," he said.
"What?"
"That's a pretty name."
"Thank you."
"We're formal again."
"Yes."
He had to slow down; he was tight and the speed had inched up.
I won't touch her, he thought. As long as I don't touch her everything will be all right.

And Marianne was remembering Tom Herbert and the baby she had not had and because she was, she was thinking that as long as she didn't let this dark-haired man touch her, everything would be all right.

CHAPTER 8

"I generally like my music wilder," Sally Talent said.
Al Leeds turned from the record player to look at her. She was lying on the couch. Her skirt had fallen back to the middle of her thighs and she had loosened her hair so that it fanned out on the cushion under her head.
"There's a time for swinging and a time for introspection."
"You look like such an animal and sometimes you don't talk like that at all," she observed.

"Baby, for a hip chick, you seem to make the scene pretty good."

"That sounds more like they way you look."

He looked out the window. "I was glad to see Cannon and your friend take off."

"With the hints you were dropping, what choice did they have?"

"I wonder what they're doing down at your place?" he asked idly.

"I don't care what they're doing."

"Neither do I."

He crossed the room and sat down beside her. Gently. He touched her ankle with his fingertips and then her thigh. She tensed, but he stopped and took his hand away. He was looking over her head, as if he were thinking about something, and she started to speak to him, but he said, "What are you doing in school?"

"I'm studying."

"No."

"Why not?"

"I don't know, but you're too hip and you know too much to be a college girl."

She laughed at him. "That's what I am, though."

He leaned over suddenly and kissed her on the mouth. It surprised her and she tried to pull away, but he held her and she put her arms around him and pulled herself up to meet him. When he touched her breast, she tightened against him and he could feel her fingernails.

He sat up. "College girls don't feel that way," he said.

She sighed and then she laughed and said, "Damn you."

"I have an idea about you," he murmured lazily.

"What?"

"Never mind now." He bent to kiss her again, but she twisted her head sideways.

She laughed at him again. "Don't get hungry," she said. "I want a promise from you."

"What?"

"I want to go for a ride with you on your motorcycle."

"Right now?"

"No, not right now, but later."

49

"All right."

"I'll wear tight slacks and no bra and we'll go a hundred miles an hour."

"All right," he said. "One hundred miles an hour."

He touched her ankle again and when he moved his hand up to her thigh, she didn't move. She smiled, but that was all.

"Do you like to go fast?" he said. He kept his hand gentle, but he knew that it was hard against her skin and he could feel goose pimples rising that gave her leg a rough, edgy texture.

She breathed deeply and touched his forearm. "If you're going at all," she said. "You should get there as quickly as possible."

She grabbed his wrist hard and held it and then let go and raised to kiss him.

He shoved her back and began to unbutton her blouse. "I'll do it," she said. "You turn up the music. "I'll do this."

He let her go and walked to the record player. When he turned, she had her blouse off. She reached behind her and unsnapped her bra and took it off and dropped it on the floor.

"Come here, hard man," she said.

She met him halfway and her body felt hard-muscled against him. He wanted to fold her in, to feel her yield, but she held solid against him and her mouth was open and alive against his until he could hardly breathe.

"I want the music louder," she said. "Turn it louder."

He twisted the volume and when he reached back for her, she was moving past him into the bedroom. He caught her at the doorway and she kissed him hard. He touched her naked breast with its pert pink nipple and she squeezed his hand.

Then she jerked away and said, "Come on, hard man. The music is loud and I want you." She laughed. "You want me too, don't you, hard man?"

She was teasing him and it made him angry. He pulled her toward him and this time he thought that it didn't matter if he hurt her.

50

But she went limp in his arms and he had to pick her up and lay her on the bed. Her skirt was twisted up high, around her waist, but she didn't seem to notice. She didn't take her eyes off his face.

He tore her skirt when he took it off, but she didn't say anything. She just watched him with bright, hard eyes, and her hands kept opening and closing.

He started to turn off the light before he undressed, but she said, "No." Her voice was normal and quiet, but her eyes and mouth gave her away.

When he lay down beside her, she turned onto her side and reached for him.

He held her hair and pulled her head back until he could reach her lips and her neck and when he kissed her she opened her lips.

He bent to kiss her breasts and she lay over flat and pulled him to her. Then they were kissing and stroking each other wildly and her silk-smooth naked flesh throbbed under the harsh caresses of his lips and hands until the wildness threatened to tear her apart and she guided him to the secret heart of her and they rode the blue thunder to ecstasy together.

Much later she lay on her stomach, her eyes wide open watching him, with a feral intentness.

He touched her neck and slid his hand slowly down her smooth back and flatted his palm on her bare buttocks.

"I want a drink," she said.

He tried to kiss her, but she bit him on the lip. When he sat up, swearing, she grinned and said, "I told you I want a drink."

"I ought to hit you," he threatened.

"Go ahead."

"I'll get you a drink instead."

She stretched and sat up beside him. "I'll be waiting right here," she said.

When he was in the kitchen, he could hear her humming tunelessly.

He mixed the drinks and brought them back to the bedroom. She took hers and scooted over on the narrow bed to make room for him. She started to say something, but he kissed her.

"Drink," he said then. "You're going to need strength to stand what I'm going to tell you."

She laughed and said, "It's all that bad?"

"Worse."

She drank a swallow of the liquor. "Okay. What?"

"Finish it." He reached backwards and set his untouched drink on the dressing table.

She looked at him curiously and handed him her glass, too. "Put it away," she said. "I don't need it."

He took hold of her by the shoulders and pushed her flat back on the bed. He kissed her and said, "Have you ever loved anyone?"

"No. Not really, I haven't."

"Neither have I, but I think I'm going to love you." She started to laugh, but he put his hand over her mouth. "Listen," he said, "I've never said that before and if you laugh at me I'll beat hell out of you."

When he took his hand away, she caught it and kissed it and then raised to kiss his mouth.

He could feel desire started again, but he wasn't ready for that yet and he tried to ignore it, though the sight of her nakedness, her smooth flanks, high arching breasts and moist red mouth was a clarion call in his blood.

He liked this girl; she had a wildness and recklessness in her that appealed to him. But he didn't love her and he knew he didn't. He wasn't going to love anyone.

But he knew what he had started. And he had a good idea that after they had made love again, she was going to remember what he had said and she was going to start thinking that maybe she did feel a beginning of love for him.

There are tricks to making a woman love you and Al Leeds knew nearly all of them.

He was taking a chance; Stone was going to raise hell about this, but it didn't matter. Stone wasn't the boss and he didn't have all the brains.

This chick could be useful. Get her planted in the store, get someone inside who could make a minute-by-minute timetable for them, and nothing could possibly go wrong.

Part of his mind was detached, but the body of the woman was soft and white and ready and willing and it had been a long time since he had touched naked woman flesh. He gave himself up to sensation and he thought about what it was she was doing to him with her hands. He heard her cry out, "Oh God," and he answered her without realizing it, pulling her hard against him while her eager body adjusted itself to him and they slid into the rhythm and ritual of love.

She lay tight against him and she said, "I think I'll do it."

"All right," he said carefully. He touched her hair. "You don't have to."

They had loved each other until they were sated and then he had told her about the plan to rob the department store.

"I knew you were a hard guy, but I didn't know how hard."

"You don't have to get mixed up with me."

"I want to," she said, twisting to look at him. "I like the caper, hard man. It sounds exciting as hell."

"It could be dangerous."

"I don't care." She laughed and rolled way from him. "I think I'm going to love you too, hard man, and I don't care how dangerous it is."

He felt good.

And what the hell. Maybe after this was over, he and Sally could make it together for a while. Until they got tired of each other.

Fran Novak held up a nightgown and said, "How do you like that?"

Jack Cannon grinned and said, "I'll have to see you in it before I can give you an opinion."

"That'll be the day."

"It was just an idea."

She laughed and put it down. "I didn't come in here for that," she said. "But I just thought I'd test your reflexes."

53

"Listen," Cannon said. "You go on and do your shopping. I think I'll wander over into the men's department and see what they have."

"What's the matter? Does all this sexy stuff upset you?"

He laughed at her. "I guess it does," he said. "So my reflexes must be all right."

Now that he was here, he wasn't sure just how to go about doing the job that Stone had sent him to do. It wasn't hard to see that there were two ways into the office; both of them were marked with large red signs. They said, PRIVATE. EMPLOYEES ONLY.

A saleman said, "Can I help you, sir?"

"I wouldn't mind looking at your suits."

They walked toward the rack together. "I think you'll find that our selection is large and in excellent taste and style."

Cannon let the saleman put a jacket on him.

"Take a look in the mirror. It fits you excellently."

Everything was excellent. Cannon wanted to laugh at the little man. "It seems all right," he said.

"Would you care to try on the trousers?"

"No. First let's see what else you have." A woman walked by. She was wearing shorts and a halter. Cannon said, "Look at that, would you."

The saleman grinned and looked less like a squirrel intent on gathering nuts. "You should see some of them," he said. "There's something about a shopping center store that makes them think they can come in half naked."

"It must be fun to work here."

"It has its good points," the salesman admitted with a grin.

"So did she."

The little man seemed to relax and want to talk. "I enjoy it here," he said.

"Open as many hours as you are, you must get tired of it."

"No, not really."

"What time do you close up at night?" Cannon queried idly.

"We lock the doors at nine, but we let anyone already in stay as long as they like."

"It must take you quite a while to get ready to leave, doesn't it?"

"No. We get out pretty early. The assistant manager comes around at eight-thirty and checks out the registers, so there isn't much money in them when we close. It doesn't take long that way to get cleared out for the night."

Cannon leaned against a table. "I remember when I was in college, I worked for a department store like this. Our manager was a bug on enthusiasim. None of us would dare leave before he was ready to go."

"Our boss isn't like that. He and the assistant are here sometimes until ten o'clock, but we can get out as soon as we're ready."

"Well, someone has to stay and check the money."

The salesman laughed. "I think they wade in it or something. But they're supposed to be getting it ready to take to the bank. They make a night deposit every evening."

"Don't the cops escort them or anything?"

"No. There really isn't any need for it. This is a quiet neighborhood."

Cannon looked at the suit rack again. He wanted more information, but he didn't know exactly what. The salesman was a lonely type, anxious to talk to people, but Cannon didn't know what else to ask.

"Let's take another look at a suit for you," the salesman said.

"No, I don't think so today."

"I have some beauties."

"Tell you the truth," Cannon said, "I'm just killing time until a woman gets through buying things over there. It makes me nervous to see all those women spending money."

"They can do it all right." The salesman had lost interest. He was too professionally polite to just walk away, but he was looking around, trying to find a customer who had money to spend.

"You go ahead," Cannon said. "I'll just wait for her."

He walked toward the back of the store and he tried to

think of what other information Stone might want him to get, but without getting inside the office there was nothing more he could do.

Leeds was right, though. Only two men would be watching the money, and there would be no police. It would be a real set-up.

He tried to think about what it would feel like to walk in here with a gun in his hand, but it only made him feel as if he were Jesse James or somebody and that made him laugh at himself.

He found Fran Novak at the water cooler.

"I've been looking at suits," he said.

"I can't picture you in a suit. What do you look like?"

"Like an executive."

"You look too much like a football player."

"I couldn't sell insurance if I didn't look like a football player."

She squeezed his bicep. "What big arms you have, Mr. Wolf."

"All the better to clobber you with."

"Are you going to hit me?" she asked in mock dismay.

"I'm thinking about it."

They joked as they walked through the store and she stopped at several counters and did some more shopping, but his mind was on the store.

He knew the layout of the sales floor. And he was nervous. This was the first time that the robbery had been more than something to laugh about. But he wasn't going to back out. He had promised Stone. But he knew he would feel a whole lot better about things if he could get into the office. Hell, maybe it double locked and they wouldn't be able to get in. The two men inside could just laugh at them and call the police.

He had the same feeling in his stomach that he used to get just before a football game. When he thought about that, the butterflies disappeared. It made him smile. He was always right after things began to move. As soon as the whistle blew for the kickoff.

He began to watch Fran as she walked ahead of him. The slacks fit tightly and her buttocks jiggled provocatively when she walked.

CHAPTER 9

Marianne was still wearing her white uniform when she left the hospital. A wisp of hair was hanging down across her face but she didn't look tired. Her shoulders were erect and she walked quickly.

Burt Stone was waiting for her at the bus stop. She was looking down at the ground, thinking about something, but he stepped into her path and said, "Hello, Marianne."

She looked up, startled, but then she smiled and said, "Hello, Burt. What are you doing here?"

"Waiting for you."

"Waiting for me?" Her eyes registered surprise but no particular pleasure.

"I would have come into the hospital, but I was afraid I'd miss you. I figured you'd be out here at the bus stop sooner or later."

She had stopped smiling. "Here I am," she said. "What did you want?"

"Nothing. I just thought maybe we could go out somewhere."

She looked down at her uniform. "Like this?"

"To a drive-in restaurant then."

"I don't think so."

"Why not?"

"That's a pretty blunt question."

"I guess so." He looked down the street. "There's no bus coming."

"There will be."

"I have the car."

She hesitated. "I'd prefer to go on home."

"I'll take you home," he offered doggedly.

"No."

"Why not?"

"I don't think I have to answer that."

"Well why not? I'll take you home if that's what you want. Why ride a bus?" He was tense now and a little angry.

"I just want to."

"Okay," he said. "Forget it. I must stink or something."

"No."

"But I'm not good enough for you."

"I didn't say that." Her cheeks flushed with color.

"You don't have to." He motioned toward the hospital. "All the doctors. Why go out with a bartender."

She looked away.

"Isn't that right?" he demanded.

"You go to hell," she retorted.

"Forget it," he said. "I'm sorry I asked."

He walked past her and out of the streetlight's circle of light, but she called, "Wait," and he stopped and turned. She had one hand to her face and she was watching him.

"What do you want?" he said.

"Come back."

"Why?"

"Please."

He went back to her, but when he stopped beside her and looked at her, his face was still flushed and angry.

"All right," she said. "I'll go with you."

"Never mind."

"Damn you," she said. "I want to go."

"I can tell that."

"I want to."

He shook his head, but then he said, "All right. The car is parked up in the next block."

He wanted to just walk away from her, to leave her there, but he turned and started toward the car. She followed him and caught up with him. They didn't touch each other and they didn't speak until they reached the car and he said, "Here it is." He was going to open the door for her, but she did it herself.

She had lighted a cigarette by the time he walked around to the driver's side and she was looking straight ahead. He started the engine without speaking to her and because he was still angry, the tires squealed when he pulled away from the curb.

He turned away from High Street and drove East until he hit the Westerville Road and then turned North. They hadn't spoken to each other since getting into the car, but she finally rolled down the window and threw away her cigarette and said, "Why did you come after me?"

"I don't know."

"I was surprised."

"No, you weren't."

She glanced at him, sharply angry, but he was looking at the road so she just said, "I guess not."

"So you know why I came after you."

"Yes."

"Why wouldn't you come with me then?"

"Because I wanted to so badly."

He slowed the car and looked at her, his features puzzled. "What?"

She didn't answer and she turned to look out the window so that he could not see her face.

"There's the trailer park," he said. She looked, but when he drove past, she didn't say anything.

She took another cigarette from the pack in her pocket and lit it before she said, "Where are we going?"

"To a motel."

"No."

"So get out."

"You said you'd take me home."

"I will."

"God damn you," she said slowly.

He looked at her and laughed. "And you, too," he said. "Why?"

"Because I want you," he said. "I wish I could tell you to go to hell and never see you again, but I can't."

"I won't go," she said.

"I told you to get out then."

"Stop the car."

"I'll stop the car when I get to the motel."

He wanted to drive a hundred miles an hour. He felt

exhilarated. Probably he could fly if he could just figure out how to lower the flaps on the car. And in a way he wished she would cry and scream and get hysterical. It was crazy, what he was doing and he knew it. He hadn't planned to do it, he had intended to take her home. It had just happened. They reached the trailer park and he went past it and that was all.

She was sitting stiffly, looking at him, but she wasn't frightened. She was angry and he wouldn't have been surprised if she had suddenly attacked him.

When they came to a motel, he swung in so sharply that the car skidded slightly and he could hear gravel being thrown aside. He stopped at a lighted building.

He opened the door and then he looked back at her. "This is your chance," he said. "The keys are in the ignition. You can just drive away."

She didn't say anything. He waited, but she only looked at the keys and back up at his face, and she didn't say anything or show any emotion.

He laughed out loud and slammed the door behind him.

There was a young man at the desk in the office. He looked as if he were probably a college boy, working at night. He was about nineteen and he wore his hair crewcut.

"I want a double room," Stone said.

"For you and your wife?"

"Yes."

"Is she really your wife?"

All the high exultant feeling suddenly drained out of Stone and he felt cold and angry and he wanted to smash something. He said, "What the hell do you care?"

"I got my orders from the boss."

"Tell the boss I said he could go to hell."

"Well, usually we ask the woman to come in, too."

"Not this time."

"I got a room with twin beds."

Stone leaned across the counter and pointed his finger at the boy. "Listen, punk," he said. "I want a room and you know exactly what kind of room I want."

The boy flushed and for a moment Stone thought he was

going to come around the desk. He was big and he was getting angry, but Stone just stepped back and watched him. He hoped the kid would come out. He wanted to hit something.

"All right," the boy said. He reached behind him and found a key. "Cabin ten. It's down to the left."

He threw the key and Stone caught it. "Thanks," he said. "How much?"

"Eight bucks."

Stone fished a ten dollar bill out of his wallet. "Keep the last two," he said. "You've been very kind and helpful."

"Wise guy," the kid said. "I hope you get a dose."

Stone turned and walked out.

Marianne was still sitting in the car. He got in and started the engine. "I thought you'd be gone," he said.

"No." Her voice was tight and strained and there was a strange brightness in her eyes.

He backed the car around and headed it toward the cabins. "Number ten," he said.

"There it is."

"That kid."

"Which one?"

"In the office there. He wanted to know why my wife didn't come in, too."

"What did you tell him?"

"That it was none of his business." He parked the car and turned it off. "All right," he said.

She opened her door.

"Listen," he said. "I'm sorry."

"For what?"

"For this."

She got out and walked to the cabin door and was waiting for him there. He unlocked the door and she went in ahead of him.

Now he felt tired, as if the argument with the kid had burned him out.

He turned on the light. The cabin was small, but there was room for a double bed, a dresser, and a television set. A bathroom was to the right of the door.

Marianne stood beside the bed and turned to face him.

He wanted to say something to her, but he was tired and all he could do was look at her.

"No big rape scene?" she asked, watching him with a strict attention.

"I said I'm sorry."

"Don't say it again."

"All right."

She looked around the room and then she said, "I'm going into the bathroom."

He stood aside and let her pass and he didn't touch her. She closed the door and locked it. He heard the bolt.

Well, all right, he thought, I wasn't going to come in. He lit a cigarette and walked to the bed. There was no chair in the room so he sat on the bed and smoked and listened to the sounds she was making. She didn't sing and all he could hear was a muffled bump now and then as she moved around and he heard the shower come on.

He lay down on the bed and put one arm under his head. Burt Stone, he said to himself, you're the world's prize idiot. This is a stupid thing to be doing. I told Jack and Al and now look at me. The last of the big time hoods, done in by a dame. Hell. The first woman I see I get the hots for.

He heard the shower stop. Then the door was unlocked and he heard her say, "Burt, come here." She sounded frightened. "Burt."

She was holding a towel, but she hadn't used it. The water was running off her naked body and making a pool on the floor. Her makeup was gone and her hair was wet and curly.

"What's the matter?" he said.

"You haven't touched me," she said. "We haven't kissed each other or even held hands or anything."

His stomach twisted. She looked so young and small and fragile that he thought for an instant he would cry for her.

"Touch me," she said. "Just touch my face or something."

Tenderness, he thought. My God, don't we forget what it is.

He stepped to her and took her face in his hands. Her skin felt slick because it was wet. She closed her eyes and with his fingers he touched them gently. Then he raised her chin and kissed her on the mouth. Very softly.

She dropped the towel, but he picked it up and began to dry her. She stood still and he rubbed her body briskly until her skin was dry and pink. He thought he should laugh, but it wasn't funny. Her body was so beautiful, it made his breath come hard. Her neck was long, finely arched and she had good shoulders. The sight of her naked breasts, full and ivory-tinted, the sleek lines of her thighs, the wide sweep of her hips was breath-taking.

He turned her around and took her in his arms and kissed her on the mouth. He kissed her hard this time and she put her arms around his neck and kissed him back and he picked her up and carried her into the bedroom.

"You haven't fixed the bed," she said.

"What?"

"Put me down."

He set her on her feet and watched while she folded back the cover. It made her look like a wife, he thought. She was naked and all women look funny when they're naked. Not funny, but from the back, when they stand barefooted, their hips appear so round, and they all look so surprisingly short.

He touched her shoulder and twisted her to face him and he kissed her again. Then he took her breasts gently in his hands, stroking them, delighting in their soft texture. "So beautiful," he murmured, and his voice shook.

"So are you," she said. "Take off your clothes."

She lay on the bed and watched him and he expected to be embarrassed, but he wasn't. He just took off his clothes and it wasn't such a big deal.

He lay beside her and he touched her, but he couldn't feel any excitement. Everything was so unreal, like something he was watching. He wanted her. God, how he wanted her. But he couldn't seem to move.

He touched her hair. It was still damp and it felt cool.

Then she sat up and looked down at him. She bent to kiss him and then she leaned down farther and kissed his stomach.

It made all the locked up desire for her explode and when

he touched her again he knew his hands were hard and must hurt her, but she only groaned once and then she locked her hands on his hair and pulled him toward her.

He felt wild now, as if all the frustration and resentment and nervousness could be poured out into her.

She cried out and he thought he had hurt her but she kept pulling him down into her until he thought he was lost and would never find his way back.

Then he heard her crying, "Now, now, now," but he couldn't listen because all the hurting was leaving him and all he could think of was the incredible depth and softness and yielding wonder of her.

CHAPTER 10

"There he is," Jack Cannon said. "He's going to be plenty pissed off."

"Man, I don't give a damn," Al Leeds said. "It's a good idea and you know it."

"Okay, but you know what he's going to say."

"Hell, I don't know. We haven't seen much of him lately."

"Maybe not, but he hasn't changed any."

Burt Stone came into the trailer, swearing. "I'm going to break my damn leg on those bumps in the road," he said.

"Where you been?" Jack Cannon said.

"To a movie."

"In the middle of the afternoon?" Al Leeds said.

"Why not? I like movies and I work nights." He had been having lunch with Marianne, but that was none of their business.

"We want to talk to you," Leeds said.

"Not now. I need a shower and I've got to get to work."

"Yes, now. You're not making a career out of tending bar and we have better things to talk about."

Stone looked at him and then at Cannon. "Okay," he said and sat down on the couch. "Go ahead."

"We want to know when the job is going to be."

"Within a month."

"Okay, fine, but we don't know enough about the store yet."

"Jack did all right, looking the place over."

"But we don't know about the office," Cannon said, breaking in. "We don't know how it's laid out, whether the money will be locked up. We don't even know that we can get into the office."

"We'll get in."

"How do you know?"

"Hell," Stone said, "we don't have to get in even. We can wait outside the office until they come out."

"Maybe they go out a back way. We don't know."

"Maybe a lot of things. We'll take the chance."

"We don't have to take any chances."

"So why don't you go over there and tell them that you'd like to see their safe and security arrangements? Tell them we're planning a robbery and don't want anything to go wrong."

"Goddamn it," Leeds said. "Why don't you listen, man?"

"He's got an idea," Cannon said. "I think it's all right."

"I am listening."

"We need a fourth person."

"We don't need him and we don't have him."

"We need a woman," Leeds said, "someone who can get a job there."

"A woman?" Stone said. "You've lost your ever lovin' mind."

"No, man," Leds said, leaning closer. "Listen. If we have an inside contact, nothing can possibly go wrong. You've worked it out pretty well, but there's still a chance. This way, bam. Everything goes like clock work."

"Forget it," Stone said. "We don't need a woman."

"Come on, Bert," Cannon said. "It makes sense to me."

"No."

"We say yes," Leeds said.

"Who the hell are you going to get?"

"Let me worry about that."

Stone stood up. "Just forget it," he said. "We don't

need a partner and we sure as hell don't need a women in."
He looked at Leeds. "You's pushing, Leeds, but just forget
it."

"We can use her."

"Who?"

Sally Talent came to the doorway of the bedroom and
said, "Me."

Stone stared at her for a few seconds, then he looked
at Leeds. "What the hell is this?" he said.

"She's in, Burt."

"I said no."

"She knows all about it. What are you going to do?"

"Forget it."

Sally walked closer and she laughed at him. "You can't
forget it. I'm in. I'll get a job there. I'll drive the car.
I'll hide the guns. Anything you say. But I'm in."

"Al," Stone said. "You dumb bastard."

"So where the hell were you the other night?"

"None of your goddamn business and I didn't bring
her into this."

"You're talking hard," Leeds said.

"And you're acting stupid."

They started toward each other, but Cannon stepped
between them and shoved them back.

"Jesus Christ, Jack." Stone said. "Why'd you let him
do it?"

"I think it's a good idea, too. She can be a help."

Stone started to say something, but he looked at Sally
and just turned away.

"She's in," Leeds said.

"Okay," he said then. "There's nothing I can do."

"That's what I said," Sally laughed. "I'm in."

"You're going to be in jail on your ass if anything
happens," Stone said. "This is no party."

"I can handle myself."

"And Leeds, too, apparently."

"Shut up," she said, her voice sharp with irritation.
"You mind your business and I'll mind mine."

"Come on," Cannon said again. "We're all in this now
and it's not going to do any good to fight each other."

"Okay," Stone said. He started toward the back of the trailer and then he turned and said, "The top third is still mine. If you guys want her in so bad, cut her in on your shares. I still get a third."

He expected an argument, but Leeds said, "Okay, man. We'll take care of her."

It was stupid, he thought as he undressed for the shower. He knew it was stupid and they should have known, too. What the hell did they need her for?

Leeds, he thought. Leeds is looking for trouble with me. I can see it. He's pushing. That's why he brought the girl in. Maybe he wants to be the leader. Hell, let him. I don't care. All I want is the money. Then Leeds and his little piece can go to hell.

But Cannon, he thought. Cannon wants her in, too. Maybe they're right. Maybe she can help.

But it made him nervous and now he thought that they had better hurry. The quicker things happened, the less chance there would be that something could go wrong.

So if we have her, he thought, we'll use her.

When he was naked, he walked deliberately back into the front of the trailer. He wanted to shock her, insult her, to make her say something foolish.

"Okay, chick," he said. "See if you can get a job over there. If you can't, make sure that you at least get into the office once. I don't give a damn if you have to get arrested for shoplifting. Get into that office."

She looked at him insolently, up and down, and then she said, "Okay, boss man, I'll handle it."

Leeds and Cannon laughed.

It made him angry, but later, in the shower, he had to admit to himself that she was a cool chick. And maybe she was less likely to mess things np than he had thought.

But he still didn't like it.

They held hands when they left the theater in the basement of Derby Hall.

It made Stone feel young to see the students as they went past him. Marianne looked as if she could be one of the college girls and it made him wish that he could back things

67

up and start all over. He remembered how good he used to feel when he was in school and thought it wouldn't be long until he was Dr. Burton Stone.

"Wasn't the play good?" Marianne said. "I thought it was wonderfull."

It was fine," he said.

"Sometimes these college productions surprise me."

He nodded. They were walking across the campus in front of the library and just ahead of them he could see a group of people sitting on the grass by Mirror Lake.

"Where would you like to go now?" he said. "I understand there's a place called the Dugout."

"I've heard of that. But I don't think I'm in the mood for anything that loud tonight."

"All right. What then?"

"Let's just drive."

He liked that. He wanted quiet, too, and he just wanted to be with her. But he hadn't wanted to suggest it. He hadn't even wanted to have a date with her; he wanted to forget her. He knew that he shouldn't be having anything to do with a woman. God knows it was bad enough that Leeds and Cannon had brought in that Sally, but he should be smart enough to avoid women himself.

Even if everything goes off well, he thought, I want to get into medical school, not get married and raise kids I can't support.

Married. That's a hell of a thing! Here I am. I know I shouldn't even be seeing her and I'm thinking of getting married.

When he took her home after they had been to the motel, he had intended to end it there. But he hadn't been able to. They sat in the car outside her trailer and they didn't talk much, but he couldn't keep from touching her. It wasn't sex, it was just softness. He wanted to feel her skin and hair and then later he wasn't able to keep from calling her.

He had lunch with her twice and four days after they had been to the motel, he went to her trailer in the afternoon when Sally and Fran weren't there and they made love again. He had planned to leave it at that, but instead he called her and asked her to go out with him on her night off from the hospital.

He was smart enough to know that his problem was needing someone to love him. He had read that everyone needs someone to love, but he knew it was more important to be loved. A man can only depend on his own ego for so long and then he has to have someone else tell him what a man he is and Burt Stone knew he needed Marianne for that.

And it was odd, he thought, the way she had changed toward him. She was still cold and withdrawn on occasions. Sometimes it seemed that she didn't want to be with him and yet couldn't draw back—as if she were waiting for him to come to her, and dreading what would happen when he did.

"Here's the car," he said.

He held the car door open for her. She watched 'm as he walked around to the driver's side and when he got in, she kissed his cheek.

"Thank you," she said.

"For what?"

"For a nice evening."

"Is it over?"

"No, but I just wanted to thank you now."

He thought that was strange. She was so serious, but there didn't seem to be anything to say to that, so he just started the engine.

They drove on Riverside Drive. It was dark there, except for the lights of oncoming cars. She sat close to him and put her head on his shoulder and when he turned on the radio, she hummed along with the music.

He didn't put his arm around her, but he could smell her hair when he leaned closer to her. He thought it smelled musky sweet, like the wind just before a rain starts to fall, and he wondered what she did to it to make it that way.

There were cars parked off the highway, near the river, and he looked at them and envied the college students in them. Everything was so new to them and they hadn't had time to get tired or disillusioned. Then he had to smile at himself for being dramatic.

Marianne thought: I have to stop this. I can't love this man.

He frightened her. After he brought her home that night, she hadn't been able to sleep. She lay awake even though she was exhausted and it made her shake to remember the way he had been. For her there had only been Tom Herbert and that other one briefly, but neither of them had been so strong or so arrogantly virile.

With both of them she had had the feeling that she was the victor, that she had beaten them, and while she never thought of them as anything but perfectly masculine, she always considered female sexuality to be ultimately stronger than any maleness. It only seemed logical. But Burt Stone had been stronger than she and while he was gentle enough with her, she could sense a power within him that scared her.

She didn't want to love him. But then she thought that maybe it didn't matter what she wanted. Maybe she was going to love him anyway and it frightened her to think that she couldn't control herself any better than that. She didn't even know anything about Burton Stone. She asked him, but he just said he graduated from New York University and then went into the army. It didn't make sense that a man like that would be a bartender. She didn't feel any snobbery about that, but it puzzled her.

And he looked so lost all the time, as if there were something worrying him. Sometimes she would think that he didn't even know where he was, that if she touched him it would startle him.

She hadn't wanted to go out with him. But when he called her, she was shaking and she said she would go out with him. She didn't want to love him, but when she looked at him she couldn't help it.

Nurse, heal thyself, she thought and it made her smile.

There were things about him she didn't like, things she didn't like because she didn't understand them. He was hard in a way she had never seen before. Al Leeds was tough, but Burt Stone was harder. And sometimes she still bristled with anger when he looked at her because he made

70

her feel that she had to defend herself against something and she didn't know what.

He reminded her of a coiled steel spring. Unloose it and it explodes its full strength and then lies spent, finished with what it was meant to do, but still quivering with strength that can be tensed again anytime. Direct, strong and irresistible once it was released.

And it frightened her to think of being in the way of it.

"Where are we going now?" she asked.

"Nowhere. Just driving."

She giggled. "Do you know what all those people in cars there are doing?"

"What?"

"They say they pull off the road there, up there by the trees where they can see the river, because they want to watch the submarine races."

He slowed the car immediately and swung off the road.

"Are we going to watch the races?" she said.

"Why not? They sound exciting."

He pulled up between two trees, a few yards from the next car and when he had turned off the lights he looked at her and said, "You are beautiful."

"Am I?"

"You know you are."

"I suppose so."

He laughed out loud. "I'm glad you said that. It would have disappointed me if you'd been modest about it."

"I wouldn't want to disappoint you."

"You couldn't."

"I could say the wrong thing."

"No, you couldn't."

She looked out toward the water. "I don't see any submarines. I wonder who's winning."

"We are."

"Are we?"

Then he laughed again and said, "You know, people say the damnedest, most stupid things, and because they're falling in love, everything sounds so romantically charged with meaning."

"Are we falling in love?" she whispered, her face very white in the darkness.

"I don't know. Are we?"

"I don't know either."

He hesitated and looked past her at the other cars parked beyond them. "I wonder if everyone here is talking the way we are."

"Probably."

A car pulled off the highway and drove toward them. "Here comes a new racing enthusiast," Stone said.

The car stopped and a man got out. He walked to their car and shone a flashlight in the window.

"What the hell are you doing?" Stone said.

"I'll ask the questions, buddy," the man said.

"Get that goddamned flashlight out of my eyes."

The light flicked to Marianne, moved over her and then went out.

"You bastard," Stone said. He opened the car door.

The man said, "I'm a cop, buddy. You'd better move on."

"Why should I?"

"Don't argue with me. Just get moving." He walked away, toward the other cars.

"Stay here, Burt," Marianne pleaded.

"What the hell's the matter with him?"

"He was disappointed that I had my clothes on."

"What?"

"They come up here and try to catch the students doing something. Then they charge them with indecent exposure."

"Fine. Somebody ought to hit that bastard in the mouth." Then he began to laugh. "Indecent, hell," he said.

She laughed with him and the longer they thought about it, the funnier it became.

They left then and went to Howard Johnson's to have something to eat before they drove home. On the way back to the trailer park then, they sat close together and listened to the radio. When they drove into the park, a police car was pulling out. A man was in the back, holding a rag to his head where he was bleeding. A woman was running after it, yelling. The cop who was driving was laughing at something.

Stone said, "Here we are, a typical American community."

"I'll bet he was beating her," Marianne said, "and now she hates the police for taking him away. She probably called them."

Stone stopped the car in front of her trailer and pulled her to him and kissed her.

"Do you want to go in?" she said.

"Are Sally and Fran home?"

"I'm not sure about Sally, but Fran's in there."

"I'd rather stay out here, then."

"Don't you like Fran?"

"I like her fine, but I'd rather just talk to you."

"All right."

He kissed her again.

"Listen," she said.

"What?"

"Nothing."

"I love you too," he said.

"How did you know I was going to say that?"

"I just did."

She put her head on his shoulder, but he raised her chin and kissed her. "Do you want to go somewhere tonight?" she said.

He kissed her hard and then he said, "No, not tonight. Tomorrow. The next day. Every day. But tonight we're having a date and I think maybe we're falling in love."

"All right," she murmured. She trembled and she put her face down against his chest so he couldn't look at her eyes.

God, he thought. I don't want to say those things. They just come out. I don't want to fall in love.

CHAPTER 11

Sally Talent was drunk.

She was in a tavern, a block from the trailer park, and she was sitting in a booth. Al Leeds was across from her. He was wearing black pants and motorcycle boots and a white polo shirt and he was sitting so that he was leaning against the wall and had one leg propped into the booth seat. He was staring at a man who had been looking at Sally because she was wearing very short shorts.

"Will you let me see you drive?" she said.

"I don't know that I'm going to drive."

"But you said you're going to drive in a stock car race." She had to speak very slowly to keep her words from slurring.

"I told you the man said maybe I could drive for him Sunday. He didn't say for sure."

"But you're going out there?"

"I go out there every Sunday."

"Why can't I go with you?"

"Because I wouldn't have time to stay with you and I don't want you wandering around alone."

"You won't have to worry about me."

He was half angry with her. She hadn't drunk much, but it had hit her hard. He wanted to talk to her seriously. "Listen, chick," he said. "I'll take you out there some time, but not this Sunday."

The man at the bar got up to leave and Leeds said, "You owe the lady a dollar, mister."

The man turned. "What for?"

"I figure you got a dollar's worth of fun out of staring at her legs. Pay her."

"You're nuts," the man said.

"Maybe, but you'd better give her the dollar." Leeds hadn't moved, but he was staring at the man.

"Why should I give her a dollar just because I looked at her?"

"Because I don't think you should be doing her that way."

The man hesitated. Then he put his hand in his pocket and brought out a wad of one dollar bills. He jerked one loose and brought it to the table. Leeds looked at him, but the man didn't say anything. He just walked quickly out of the bar.

Sally said, "What'd you do that for?"

Leeds laughed. "Marlon Brando said that in 'One Eyed Jacks.' He said, 'Don't be doing her that way'."

"You didn't really care if he looked at me."

"Yes, I did," he said. "But mostly I just wanted to see if I could scare him out of a dollar."

She stared at him for a moment, then she began to laugh, too.

Then he said, "Now listen, try to remember what I'm saying."

"I always remember what you say."

He wanted her, he could feel desire starting deep within him. "You could make any man forget his business," he said.

"Do you like me?"

"I like you."

"Am I good?"

"The best."

"Really." She took his hand and dug her fingernails into it. "Am I the best?"

It hurt, but he didn't change expression. He just watched her and when she finally let go, there was blood oozing from the gouged marks on his hand.

"Listen," he said then. "If you ever do anything like that again, I'll beat hell out of you." He spoke quietly and evenly and he still hadn't moved his hand.

"All right," she said. "I'm listening."

"You handle that job at the store right," he said. "Don't come on like a hard type or something. Get as much information as you can, but don't attract too much attention.

Find out about the office, where they keep the money. Find out what kind of guys the manager and assistant are. I want to know in advance whether to expect a tough time."

"All right," she said again. "You've told me before. I'll work on it." She smiled then. "Would you really beat me up?"

"I don't get my kicks that way."

"But you'd do it."

"If you ever use those fingernails on me again."

"I won't."

"Then I won't have to hit you."

She laughed out loud and said, "I can't wait till we do the robbery."

"You change the subject faster than any woman I've ever seen."

"I know. It makes me charming."

"Charming, hell. You'd better keep your mind on what you're doing."

"I can handle it."

"I think so, too."

Actually, she bored him. She was sharp, but she was young, and she didn't have the animal shrewdness that really tough chicks seem to be born with. She wanted to be sophisticated and adventurous. Hell, she thought she already was. She thought she was Calamity Jane and Ma Barker combined.

But the way she looked at him. It made him tense to think of it.

She said, "Let's go some place, hard man."

"Where?"

"Where do you think."

He started to say something, but he changed his mind and leaned back. He was going to say, Look, chickie, this is a crime we're in on. They can put you in jail for it. It's only in the movies where the beautiful frail gets off because the handsome cop can tell she isn't really bad. The judge doesn't really give a shit whether you're good. God might look at the difference between bad actions and bad people, but the judge won't care. And that means twenty years where the only lovers are dykes and the only pets are cockroaches.

But he decided to hell with it. She wouldn't listen. She was all charged up. Besides, he didn't want to lose the use of her.

"Come on," she said. "Let's go."

He got up and they left the bar. He'd borrow Cannon's car and they'd go to a motel or something. What the hell? In the sack she was the best he had ever seen and by now she thought he loved her and when they were making love maybe he did. She said she loved him and that was what he had set out to make happen.

But at the moment he didn't think he could stand anymore of her making like a female Jimmy Cagney.

"Did you know that you wiggle in back when you walk?" Jack Cannon said. He was mixing drinks in the kitchen and he could see Fran Novak on the couch.

She laughed and said, "If I'd known you were going to make fun of my baby fat, I wouldn't have come down here tonight."

"Sure you would have. Everyone gone but us and here we are, two lonely people, grabbing for companionship in a cold world."

"Just as long as companionship is all you grab for."

He walked back into the room, carrying the drinks. "Now that was a nasty thing to say," he said. "I think you need a drink."

She tasted it. "It's too strong."

"Naturally."

"But I like it."

"I was hoping you would. . . ."

Fran Novak liked Jack Cannon. She didn't love him and she didn't expect to, but she liked him and so that was enough. She was of Polish extraction, second generation American, her grandfather was still alive and still couldn't speak English. But Fran grew up around big men, men who worked with their muscle, and while she had as much respect as anyone for intellect, she was never able to shake off a feeling that a real man was a big man.

She was born in Pittsburgh. Her father was a millworker. But they left there when she was four because a cousin none of them had ever heard of died and left enough money for her father to buy a garage in a small town in Indiana called Almsville. Her father had never liked working in the mill. He didn't mind it for himself, but that's what his father had done after coming to America, and Franik Novak, called Frank in Pittsburgh, was a firm believer that every generation should do just a bit better than the last. So he bought his garage and he worked hard at it and he made a success of it. He sent his daughter to business college and he sent both of his sons to the University of Pennsylvania.

Fran was proud of her father. He was a kind and gentle man despite his strength and size. If he drank too much sometimes, it wasn't often and he could afford it, and if anything, he even kinder and gentler then.

She was proud of her mother, too, but for different reasons. Her mother's laugh was what it was. She laughed deep in her throat, the way a woman should laugh when she's satisfied by her man, and if her mother hadn't been a beautiful woman, she had been a woman and Fran knew that her father's bed had never been a cold or unhappy place.

Her mother had wide hips and huge, full breasts and massive heavy thighs and she didn't speak English well. Once, when she was thirteen, Fran was ashamed that her mother didn't look like the mothers of her friends, but she grew out of that because she noticed that her father didn't look like the fathers of her friends, either, and when she compared them, she had to think that maybe her mother had a lot to do with that. She remembered once her father saw a woman on television and he said that he thought she was pretty and her mother said in Polish, "One night with you would ruin her. You need a woman, not a skinny girl." And her father had laughed and laughed and so had her mother.

That's the way she liked it. . . .

Jack Cannon laughed and said, "Man, I really did make this drink strong. I can feel the hair waving on the back of my neck."

"I can see it," she said.

"I'm a man of many talents."

"I'll bet you are."

"You sound sexy," he said, smiling gently.

"I am sexy."

"I'll bet you are."

"You're stealing my line."

"I'd like to."

She laughed and said, "I think you're making me an offer of something, but I'm not sure what it is."

"Yes, you know what it is."

"All right. I know."

"I like you."

"I like you, too."

"So why don't you kiss me then?"

"All right."

He was surprised and he hesitated, but when she laughed at him, he took her into his arms and kissed her on the mouth. He wanted her, but she had come to him so quickly that he was off balance, unsure of himself. He had one hand on her waist and he moved it toward her breast, but he would have stopped if she had not caught it and pressed it to her breast outside her clothes.

Then he kissed her again, harder, and he put his hand into the neck of her blouse, but her brassiere was tight and when he tried to put his hand into that, the strap broke.

Fran sat up without looking at him. She picked up her drink and took a swallow of it.

"You don't love me," she said.

"Yes, I do."

"Don't say that. I don't want you to say that."

"Okay," he laughed. "I don't love you, but I like you a lot."

"Do you want me? I mean, really want me. I don't mean, would you just like to go to bed. I mean, do you really want me?"

"Yes, I really want you," he said seriously.

"I want you, too," she said. "But I don't love you."

"All right."

"Anything I do, I do because I want to. And I don't like to be taken seriously."

She was so grim about it that it made Cannon laugh and she frowned, but he kissed her again and she leaned against him and this time when he put his hand inside her blouse, the strap on her bra was already broken so he was able to take her breast into his hand.

Before he knew what she was doing, she ripped open his shirt and bit him on the chest.

"Goddamn it," he said.

She laughed and said, "Goddamn it."

Then he laughed, too, and he held her down, laughing, and he took her clothes off so that she was writhing and giggling, naked on the couch, and then he picked her up easily and carried her into the bedroom.

He dumped her on the bed and said. "You play just like a puppy."

"It might as well be fun."

"It is."

"It would be even more fun if you had your clothes off, too."

She lay still while he undressed, but when he tried to lie down beside her, she rolled over and sat up and began to tickle him.

"Hey," he said. "Stop it."

"You don't have me yet," she said.

It made him half angry and he sat up and grabbed her, but she was strong and she fought him hard. She was laughing all the time, but she was fighting.

It excited him. He didn't want to hurt her, but it excited him and he forced her back flat and held her.

"All right," she said, "come on." She was panting and she was laughing, her eyes bright, her body singing with passion. When he entered her, she gave a little cry, then clutched him tight to her, reveling in the riot of sensation that assailed her.

They smoked cigarettes together, on the narrow bed, and he stroked her naked body gently. He thought it was strange to see how quiet she was now. She watched him and she smiled when he spoke to her, but she lay motionless, as if she were very sleepy.

"You know," she said. "You're a nice man."

That made him laugh. "I think you're a nice lady, too," he said.

"It's sort of funny to meet you here."

"You mean in bed here?"

"No. In a trailer camp."

"What's wrong with a trailer camp?" he asked, genuinely puzzled.

"Nothing. But you just don't seem to fit here."

"And you do?"

"No. Marianne and Sally and I didn't know what we were getting into when we came here. We were just looking for an inexpensive place to live. We didn't know that none of our friends would come out here because you know what kind of girls live in trailer parks."

"I don't know whether I'm being insulted or complimented," he said.

"Neither one. I just wondered why you and your friends picked a trailer camp."

"Maybe for the same reason you did."

"No. You've been around more. You knew about trailer camps. Do you know there's a whorehouse—whoretrailer— just up around the circle?"

"No, I didn't know that."

"Two women. They work until they get chased out. Then they just move their trailer to another park."

"I'll be damned," he said.

"So why are you living in a trailer?"

"To save money."

"Three young bachelors living together don't have to pay that much rent," she pointed out.

"More than here."

"Besides, you three all intrigue me. Burt is hardly the bartender type and Al Leeds sure doesn't look like a television salesman to me. And that company you're selling insurance for. You could sure do better."

He laughed. "Maybe we just don't like responsibility."

"So be mysterious," she said.

"There isn't any mystery. Three guys get out of the army. That's all."

"All right," she said. "Be mysterious, I don't care." And she really didn't. It wasn't any more than curiosity. She liked to analyze people; she considered it a hobby. But there was something illogical about the three men and she wondered what it was.

CHAPTER 12

Sally Talent liked the way she looked when she was naked.

Her body was still wet from the shower she had just taken and she was standing outside the stall shower, looking at herself in the mirror on the door.

She turned now to look at her body in profile.

Marianne Nirvell was sitting on the bed, brushing her hair. "Every woman comes with the same equipment," she said sharply.

"Not equipment like this," Sally retorted.

"Maybe not."

"You're damned right not."

"You sound proud of yourself."

"Shouldn't I be?"

"I suppose."

Sally stepped back from the mirror and said, "What's the matter?"

"Nothing." Marianne put down the hairbrush. "Are you going out?"

"Yes."

"With Al Leeds?"

"Of course with Al Leeds. Who else have I been going out with."

"Are you coming home tonight?"

Before she thought, Sally said, "Early tonight. Al's driving in that race tomorrow. He wants to get to bed early." Then she said, "What do you mean, am I coming home tonight?"

"I mean, I think Al's been getting to bed early for several nights now."

"Say what you mean."

"You've been having an affair with him, haven't you?"

"I haven't been having an affair with anyone."

"I think you have," Marianne insisted.

"I don't care what you think."

"I don't suppose you do."

"Then leave me alone." Sally's eyes flashed angrily and her voice had a cutting edge to it.

"Sally, I just want to help you," Marianne said.

"Jesus Christ!"

"Don't talk that way."

"Why not?" Sally put her hands on her hips. "Who do you think you are to be talking to me that way? I don't think you and Burt Stone have just been talking."

"No, we haven't been talking."

"Then you don't have any right to preach at me."

"I'm not preaching at you."

"What are you doing then?"

"Sally." She hesitated. "Al Leeds is older than you are."

"Not much."

"Years and years the way it counts. Men like Al are born older than you'll ever be."

"Don't sound like a soap opera."

"Well, what makes you think you can handle Al Leeds. That's a man, Sally. You're used to boys."

"What makes *you* think you know what I'm used to?"

Sally started to turn away, but Marianne stood up and held her arm. "Listen," she said. She tried to keep her voice from cracking. "What happens if you get pregnant? Do you think Al Leeds is going to marry you? And even if he would, is he the man you want for a husband?"

Sally began to laugh. "Now what makes you think I want a husband at all?" she said.

"Every woman wants a husband and family."

"I don't. I want excitement and laughs."

"What if that adds up to a baby."

"Don't be stupid."

Marianne stared at her and she was going to slap her, but Sally jerked her arm away and turned her back. Marianne sat down on the bed again. She felt tired and she was embarrassed now because she felt like Sally had just seen right through everything she was thinking.

She was sorry she had said anything. But Sally had looked so young, standing there in front of the mirror, and she wanted to do something for her. Al Leeds frightened her and she wanted to save Sally from him. From what? What did she know? She was on three years older than Sally and one abortion hardly makes an oracle.

"All right," she said. "Forget it all. Go on and have your fun."

She hadn't intended it, but the words were harshly sarcastic, and she wasn't surprised when Sally wheeled and said, "What do you mean by that?"

"Oh Sally," Marianne said. "What's it going to get you?"

Sally laughed. "Not what you think. I'm going to get money. Lot's of it. And Al and I aren't going to live this way much longer."

"What are you talking about?"

"Don't you wish I'd tell you?"

"No."

"You're so superior, aren't you? You think Burt Stone's so different from Al." Sally's mouth twisted in a sneer.

"He is."

"The only difference is that Al has more guts. Stone's in as deep as Al."

"As deep in what?"

Sally's face had turned a deep red and the flush had spread down over her naked breasts. "They're going to pull a robbery," she said. "And your precious little Burt is the one who thought it up."

"What?" Marianne's voice was stiff with shock and her eyes were stricken.

The anger had drained out of Sally now and her face

was white. She was holding her cheeks with both hands and she looked frightened.

"What did you say?" Marianne said.

"Nothing."

"You're lying."

"Yes, I was lying."

Marianne stood up again; she was shaking. "Were you?"

Sally looked at her, frightened and regretting her outburst but she wouldn't say anything.

"I'll ask Burt." Marianne said. "He'll tell me."

"No," Sally said. "You mustn't ask him."

"Why not?"

Most of the color had come back to Sally's face, but she still looked frightened.

"Are you afraid of what Al will do to you for telling me?" Marianne demanded.

"No," Sally said. "But it was just something I said to make you mad. You'll make us both look silly." She turned around again and began to dress hurriedly.

"Are you still going out?"

"Yes."

Marianne was surprised that she felt so calm. She left the bedroom and went into the front of the trailer and sat down. She could still see Sally, but even this far away, she felt separated and detached.

She was sure that Sally had been telling the truth. She was too frightened now to have been lying. But the queer thing was that she felt so calm. She wasn't angry or hurt. She wasn't even surprised.

Once she heard a minister say that it wasn't sex or obscenity that he objected to so strenuously in literature. He said it was the theme of fatalism. He said too much modern literature portrayed evil as something inborn in a person, as something that a man or woman could not escape no matter how badly they wanted to be good.

The minister insisted that was a pagan idea. He said the Greek drama had been centered around that idea, that what was conceived in evil would always be evil, that what was

85

once evil would always be the same, that nothing could be done to change the real inner person.

The minister said that was the real obscenity. He stated that Christianity had proved that no evil was inescapable. He said God had given man free will so that the man could make a decision, could control his fate, and he said that evil, once touched, didn't have to influence an entire life. He said that evil was always there, but he said that free will was enough to allow anyone to escape it.

He said that Christianity had proved that. He said that the idea of fate was stupid and sinful.

But she wondered if anyone believed that. She wasn't surprised at what had happened. She loved Burt Stone and she knew all along that she shouldn't. She couldn't help it. Evil calls to evil, doesn't it?

It was all so stupid. She didn't believe that.

But Burt couldn't help being what he was. None of them could.

She began to cry—dry, hacking sobs. She didn't notice when Sally went out.

CHAPTER 13

The car swung heavily, sideways, and there was a spew of hot oil that blew up from the track and hit Leeds in the face. He felt the car twisting, but there was nothing he could do. When he jerked the wheel, there was response, but he tensed because the car was leaning sharply.

But instead of bouncing over against the wall, the car spun itself out and was facing in the right direction. He jammed the stick up and he heard the tires slipping before they caught in the gravel at the edge of the track and whipped him ahead.

He was swearing and he could still taste the oil, but he leaned forward, grinning tightly. He passed two cars on the outside, but the car rocked wildly when he went around the curve that was away from the grandstand. He rode out the turn and it made him laugh out loud the way the car jumped out when it hit straight ground. It unwound, whining, and he was doing seventy by the speedometer when he slammed into the next curve. He hauled back on the wheel and the car rocked again, but it twisted across the track and he made the turn without touching the brake.

He could see the Ford ahead of him and he could see the back of the driver's head. He was yelling, but he didn't know it.

The Ford was running first, four or five lengths in front of a black Dodge, but he rammed the engine open and when he saw the next curve coming, he leaned against the door as if body English could help him get the car around, but he didn't brake, and he came out of it wide open and by the time they passed the stands, he had passed the Dodge and was in second place.

He passed the officials' box and there was a big sign with a seven on it which meant that they were going into the last two and a half mile lap.

He swore again. The car he was driving was a Chevrolet, but he was pushing it as hard as he could and he wasn't gaining on the Ford very fast.

He moved his helmet back as far as possible and then he shoved it off altogether. He was sweating and his hands felt slick, but his knuckles were white with pressure.

They went into the first curve and he had to touch the brake slightly because he was doing eighty, but he came out fast and on the inside lane. The Ford had slipped back a length and was cutting across the track so he had picked up two lengths in time. He laughed when he saw it and he shoved the gas pedal to the floor. He was holding it down as hard as he could, as if he thought he could push it through the floor and get more speed, and the pressure was making his leg cramp.

He was only two lengths back now and it was hard to see because of the other car's dust trail, but he saw the driver glance back once and that made him laugh again.

The curve was ahead of them. The driver in the Ford slowed down, but Leeds swung into the outside and caught him. He looked sideways at the other man and began to edge his car closer.

The man in the Ford yelled something, but Leeds couldn't hear him. He laughed and shouted: "Bastard!"

He thought for a second that the other driver wasn't going to break, but then the Ford slowed and dropped back and Leeds cut in short. They hit the curve and both of them skidded. The Ford went outside, and instead of holding in, Leeds wheeled with him.

They rocked toward the wall, both of them, so close together that Leeds could hear the other man yelling, but almost as if they were tied together, they twisted out and rode the curve on the bank.

They came out slowly, but Leeds was still in front. He looked in his mirror. The Ford was dropping back, deliberately slowing and falling away.

The black Dodge passed them both and Leeds forgot about the Ford then and jammed out again, but the Dodge had too much speed going into the final turn and Leeds couldn't catch him.

He finished second, three lengths back, but he didn't care. The Ford finished sixth.

He drove into the maintenance area and sat for a few minutes, listening to the engine before he cut it off. He was tired, but he felt good.

The owner of the car came running over. He was a small man, a driver himself, but his left wrist was in a sling. He stuck his head in the window and said, "What the hell were you doing? You could have won."

Leeds opened the door and got out. "I finished second," he said. "What do you want out of me?"

"You could have won."

"That son of a bitch cut me off earlier. He's lucky I didn't run him into the wall."

"Well, what the hell. You could have killed him."

"I damn well thought of it." The man started to say something else, but Leeds said, "Shut up. I won two thousand dollars for you."

"Okay," the man said. "Okay, I'll get you your seven-fifty and bring it here."

"Thanks a lot," Leeds said, sarcastic. "I'll be waiting."

Leeds watched the man leave. He didn't know why he had been hard with him. Maybe it was just a habit.

"You think you're something, don't you?"

"What?" he turned around.

"I was driving that Ford." The man was bigger than Leeds and he looked strong.

"You did a hell of a job with it," Leeds said. "I think you still could have placed if you hadn't chickened out."

"You damn fool."

"The same to you, Charley. Maybe you'll think twice before cutting a man off again."

"I didn't cut you off."

"You're a liar. You spun me out in the third lap and I almost took the wall."

"You were sneaking through. I didn't know you were coming."

"Sneak through hell," Leeds said calmly. "I saw you look back at me."

Several men had come closer and were listening. One of them grinned and said to Leeds, "Tell him, Blacky. You gave him hell out there."

Leeds grinned back and said, "I think he learned his lesson."

The other driver grabbed Leeds' shirt. "I'll kick your ass," he said.

Leeds didn't move. "Let go of me," he said.

"You're tough, aren't you?"

"I said let go of me."

"You're almost too little to fight, but I think maybe I'll just give you a good spanking."

Somebody laughed, but Leeds didn't say anything.

"Now apologize to me," the man said.

"Let go of me, you big bag of guts."

The man hesitated, but he still didn't let go. Leeds brought up his right arm in a sudden, savage blow against the man's wrist. The shirt tore loose and the man stepped back, swearing.

"All right," he said. "It's all right with me."

He stepped forward and swung wildly at Leeds' head,

but Leeds stepped in close with his head against the man's upper arm and dug his fist into the big man's belly, hard. When the man grunted and tried to grab him in a bear hug, Leeds twisted him around against the car and smashed his fist into his mouth. The man grunted again and spat blood, but before he could recover, Leeds hit him with a left hook and then again with a right. The man sagged. Leeds hit him and straightened him, then hit him again and slammed him against the car.

Leeds blasted him seven or eight more times before someone made him quit and let the man fall.

The men watching were quiet. Somebody said, "Jesus Christ," but nobody moved to help the man on the ground. Leeds wasn't panting, but his right hand hurt.

The man who owned the car he had driven stepped in front of him. "Here's your money," he said.

Leeds took it and stuffed it into his pocket.

"Now get out of here," the man said.

"What?"

"Get out of here."

"Suppose you throw me out."

Someone in the crowd said, "The other guy started it."

Leeds looked at the man who spoke and he started to say something, but then he shrugged and walked away.

Sally Talent was standing beside a truck, watching, and she called to him. He stopped to see who it was and then he waited for her.

"Are you all right?" she said.

"I hurt my hand." He laughed. "I'm all right."

"I saw the last part of the fight. What happened?"

"I was behaving like a guy who lives in a trailer camp."

She laughed out loud. "Yes, you were," she said. She laughed again, excited. "I never saw anything like that."

He stopped and looked at her. "What are you doing here? I told you I didn't want you here."

"I had to come."

"Why?"

"I did something."

"What's eating you?" Leeds demanded sharply.

"I told Marianne what we were doing," Sally said.

"What?"

"We had a fight and I told her."

"Told her what?"

"I told her about the robbery."

"When?"

"Last night. Before we went out."

"Why didn't you tell me last night?"

"I was afraid to." She looked at his face. "Well, I was. I didn't know how you'd react."

"What did she do?" Leeds asked, frowning, feeling sudden, savage disgust with her.

"She cried."

"I don't care about that. Did she call the cops?"

"No."

"Will she call the cops?"

"I don't know."

He looked out toward the track. Then he turned back and slapped her face.

"You don't know," he said.

She didn't cry. She didn't even touch the red welt his hand left.

"I warned you," Stone said.

"I know you did," Leeds admitted. "But that isn't going to help a damned bit."

"You'll have to take care of her."

"What the hell do you want me to do, put her in a barrel of cement and drop her in the river?"

"She'll call the cops."

"She doesn't have anything to tell them."

"Not yet, but she will have." Stone pushed his hand through his hair. "Damn it," he said. "Who else has this girl of yours been talking to?"

"No one."

"How do you know?"

"Listen," Leeds said. "I know. Now what are you going to do about Marianne?"

Stone looked out the window at the incinerator across

91

the driveway. Someone had put oily rags into it and a thick smoke was blowing toward them. "I'll talk to her," he said.

He waited for her at the hospital. The woman at the desk said she was due off earlier, but that she was in operating, so he sat in the downstairs lounge and waited for her. He gave the woman a message, but he was afraid she wouldn't come. He thought she would probably go out the back way.

But she came down the stairs and she had changed clothes. She saw him when she was halfway down and he stood up to wait for her.

When she reached him, he took her hand and said, "Come on." He expected her to refuse, to pull her hand away, but she tightened her hand in his and went with him.

He took her to a drive-in movie because he couldn't think of any other place where no one would bother them. On the way there, neither of them spoke, except once when Marianne asked him for a cigarette and he handed her the pack.

When they were parked, they left the speaker on the pole. He put an arm across the back of the seat and looked at the screen. "I know you know about it," he murmured.

"Did Sally tell you?"

"She told Al. He told me."

"He didn't hurt her, did he?"

He didn't answer her. The people on the screen looked funny, their mouths were moving, but he couldn't hear anything.

"Burt," she said, "what are you going to do?"

"I thought Sally told you."

"I mean now."

"I'm still going to do what Sally said."

"No."

"Yes." He looked at her; the shadows made her look thinner and older. "I have to," he said.

"Why?" she asked, her voice small and somehow pleading.

"I need money."

"No one needs money that badly."

"I do," he said. He felt very calm, as if he were an adult who was trying to explain to a child why the tragedy really wasn't a tragedy.

"You have a job."

He laughed. "A bartender," he said.

"There's nothing wrong with that."

"Yes, there is." He looked away again. "I want to do something else—something that takes money."

"How much?"

"Too much to wait until I save it up as a bartender." He turned to face her. "Did you ever have somebody take something away from you?" he said.

She said, "Yes," and she would have told him more, but he went on quickly.

"Well, I have a brother," he said, "and my brother took ten thousand dollars that belonged to me."

"Why did your brother take it?"

"He just did," he said. "What difference does that make? He just took it. He said he never even thought about it."

"What did he do with it?"

"I don't know. He bought a liquor store. Something. He aimed to pay it back, I think, but he just took my money."

"Did the money mean that much?" she asked.

"I was going to be a doctor."

"What?"

"A doctor. You know what doctors are, nurse. They wear white uniforms and they tell people to take pills."

He looked toward the screen and he thought maybe he was going to cry. He wished he could. But his eyes were dry; it was just in his throat. His throat hurt.

"I'm sorry," she said.

"Sure you are. So am I. But that doesn't add up to ten thousand dollars."

"Maybe it can."

"I worked like hell to get through undergraduate school," he said. "I didn't spend any of that money. I thought I'd need it in medical school."

"That's why you want the money from the robbery. You still want to be a doctor."

"Yes, I want to be a doctor," he said.

"Please don't do it this way." Her eyes were wide on his face. "Please, Burt, for me."

"No. For me. For Doctor Burton Stone." His voice was hard, his face implacable.

"You don't have to."

"You think I want to be a bartender all my life?"

"You could get a job in a corporation, work your way up." She was talking fast, arguing, desperately.

"You mean I could be a trainee?" His voice had hardened and it made her stop. "A trainee," he said. "That's what my brother said. Be a trainee somewhere. Get a job."

"There's nothing wrong with it."

"I want to be a doctor."

"Be a doctor then. Other men do it."

"No one works his way through medical school. It can't be done."

"Not alone maybe."

"I'm alone."

"No," she said. She began to cry.

"Well, I am," he said. He watched her and he was glad that he had made her cry. He felt that he was absolved of something, now that she was crying. He wanted to hurt her, to make her cry out, not physically, but it was almost as if he could be rid of the pain in himself by causing pain in her. He had wanted her to cry. He had been keeping his voice cold and hard so she would cry. But it all left him then and he felt sad and he touched her shoulder and then her face and he made her look at him. "Don't," he said.

"I can't help it."

"Nobody can help anything."

"Yes, we can," she said fiercely. "We don't have to get pushed into things."

"I have to do this," he said.

She was still crying, but she sat up and looked at him. "You can be a doctor," she said.

"How?"

94

"I'll help you."

"What? Do my homework for me while I go out to work?"

"No." She touched his face. "Don't you know I love you?"

"Not any more. Things are different now."

"Now I love you more."

"I love you, too."

"I know," she said. "I know."

He wanted to take her into his arms, but she stopped crying as suddenly as she had started, and she sat up straighter and said, "I'll tell you what we can do. I'll support you through medical school."

"No. I know what nurses make," he said.

"I'll make enough."

He was surprised and he didn't know what to say. As he thought about it, he didn't know why he should be surprised. Maybe it was because no one had ever loved him before, not while he was old enough to be conscious of it anyway, and he didn't know what to expect.

"It can work," she said.

"I don't want you to support me."

"It's better than going to jail."

"I don't want you to support me," he repeated.

She hesitated and looked away and said, "You don't have to marry me. That's not what I meant."

"I love you," he said.

"Please," she said.

"All right."

"You won't do it?"

"No."

"Will you tell the other two?"

"Yes."

She began to cry again and she put her face against his shoulder and shuddered when he tightened his arm around her.

Oh God, he thought, I don't know. I want to do it. But how can I tell Leeds and Jack? And how will we live, cramped up, you working? Maybe there'll be a baby. Maybe anything. Jesus.

"I'll try," he said.

"What?"

"Nothing. I love you."

He would try.

CHAPTER 14

The roses were dying.

From her chair at the table in her trailer, Marianne could see them. She had watched the little woman who lived in the next trailer plant them and at the time she thought it was a pitiable thing.

The little woman was graying and the trailer she shared with her husband was graying and the two of them had built a wooden porch onto the front of their trailer and it was graying, too. Everything was. The woman had planted the roses carefully and she tried to take care of them, but they were dying. Marianne thought it was probably because of the heavy smoke that blew over them from the incinerator across the driveway, but it didn't matter why.

Fran Novak said, "What's the matter with you and Sally? Have you been fighting?"

"No."

"Then why aren't you talking to each other? Something's wrong."

Marianne could still see Sally. She was walking toward the bus stop. She was carrying her school books.

"No, nothing's wrong," she said.

"Don't you want to tell me about it?"

"There's nothing to tell."

Fran stood up. "Okay," she said. "Excuse me for living. You want some more coffee?"

"No." She looked up. "There is something," she said. "I want to tell you."

"All right. You know I'm a good listener." Fran smiled "Let me get some more coffee. Anything is easier with more coffee."

"Sit down," Marianne insisted. Fran sat down. "They're going to do a robbery."

"Who is?"

"Burt and Al and Jack. Sally's helping them. That's why she took that job at the store. They're going to rob the store."

Fran began to laugh.

"I'm serious," Marianne said.

"Did Burt tell you?"

"Yes."

"Really?" Fran stopped laughing.

"He said he wouldn't then. We talked about it and he said he wouldn't, but I'm afraid."

"You said Burt said he wouldn't."

"They'll make him change his mind, Fran," she said.

"Is Jack in it, too?" Fran said, as if she had just then thought about it.

"Yes. They won't let Burt change his mind."

"He told you he wouldn't."

"But I made him say that."

"Do you love him?"

"Yes."

"Does he love you?"

"Yes."

"Then they won't make him change his mind. And if he backs out, they'll have to, too." Fran lit a cigarette.

"He wouldn't tell on them," Marianne said. "They could go ahead." She took a cigarette from the pack, but she didn't light it. She rolled it between her fingers. "I don't care about that, but I don't want him to do it."

Fran stood up suddenly. "I don't want Jack to do it either," she said. "But they won't now."

"How do you know? They could make him change his mind."

"Maybe they can't. Maybe he really loves you."

"He does love me, but he wants to be a doctor. That's why he wants the money."

Fran turned and walked into the kitchen. She brought the coffee pot.

"I'm sorry I told you," Marianne said. "Now you're worried, too."

"Only about you and Sally."

Marianne looked out the window again. Sally was gone from sight, but the little woman next door had come out. she was wearing only a cotton duster that gaped open when she bent over the flowers.

She felt a sudden surge of sexual desire that was so strong it made her shiver and she thought that was strange because what she had been thinking of was what it would be like to kill Al Leeds.

Al Leeds laughed and it woke up Burt Stone. He was startled and for an instant he was wide awake, like an animal, listening, but then he heard Leeds and Cannon in the front part of the trailer and he lay back, sleepy again.

He closed his eyes and tried to drop off to sleep, but they had the radio on and it kept him awake. He didn't want to get up. He rolled onto his back and looked at the ceiling.

He remembered. For a few seconds there hadn't been any robbery or Marianne or anything to worry about. But he remembered now. She was expecting him to tell them that he wasn't going to go through with the robbery. She was going to support him while he was in medical school. God!

"Hey, Burt," Leeds yelled. "Get the hell up."

"I'm asleep," he shouted back.

He wanted to do it. He thought: she's right. It would be stupid to do it. I don't have to. She's willing to help me. She loves me. But I don't want her to support me. I don't want her to give me money.

But he knew that what he really meant was, I want that ten thousand dollars; I've got it coming.

Only he didn't have it coming. His money was gone. His goddamn brother had spent his money. And there isn't any rule anywhere that says the world has to make up for what your brother steals.

And Leeds. He wasn't afraid of Leeds. He knew Cannon wouldn't cause any trouble, but Leeds might. Still, he wasn't afraid of him. That wasn't the problem. He had set them onto this. It was his idea. He was the brain, the guy who thought everything out. And then he broke his own rule and messed everything up because the first woman he touched was good in bed.

No. Not in bed, damn it. I love her. It's different than it is with Leeds and Sally.

Or is it?

"Stone," Leeds yelled again. "Come on, man. We have to talk."

He sat up on the edge of the bed and rubbed his hands through his hair. "Okay," he said. "I'm coming." He stood up and put on a pair of pants and went into the living room. They had the table set up and were drinking coffee. There was a box of Wheaties out.

He got himself a bowl and a cup and sat down at the table. "Okay," he said. "I'm up, for Christ's sake."

"It's about time."

"I was late getting in."

"Getting in where?" Leeds said.

Stone felt a flare of anger, but he poured cereal into the bowl and only said, "Getting home."

They had gone to a motel after leaving the drive-in movie and they had made love, not wildly but sadly and gently, and she hadn't said a word about the robbery. That made it hard. She had acted as if she just assumed she could trust him. He said he would do it and she thought he would. If she had picked at him, maybe he could have become angry, but she didn't say anything.

They watched him fix his cereal and then Jack Cannon said, "Come on, Burt. What'd she say?"

"She said you guys are a couple of bastards."

Leeds laughed. "We are."

"Come on," Cannon said. "What'd she say?"

"It's all right."

"What's that mean?" Leeds said.

I don't know, for Christ's sake, Stone thought. "You don't have anything to worry about."

"Everything goes off the way we planned it?"

"Yes."

99

"Wait a minute," Leeds said. "That's not enough for me. I want to know what kind of deal you made with her. She doesn't look like a woman who'll shut up just because you told her to. I want to know how you fixed it."

"I took a big needle and I sewed her lips together."

Cannon laughed nervously.

"Smart guy," Leeds said. "You got to be the big boss. Can't tell us what's going on."

"Calm down," Cannon said.

"I don't want to calm down. I want to know how he fixed it."

Stone shoved his bowl away from him. "I fixed it," he said. "That's all. I just fixed it."

"How?"

"That's none of your goddamned business."

Leeds started to get up, but Cannon jumped up first and shoved him back into his seat. "Knock it off," he said, "or I'll beat hell out of you myself."

Leeds started up again, but Stone said, "We're going to get married. That's how I did it. I said we'd get married."

Leeds stared at him and began to laugh. "Okay," he said, "that's all I wanted to know. What's the big deal you wouldn't tell me?"

Cannon sat down again. "Are you really going to marry her?"

"I guess I'll have to. Otherwise, we'll all go to jail."

They laughed and Leeds said, "That fixed it up, huh? You're going to get married so she doesn't care?"

"She likes money, too."

"Okay," Leeds said. "Now. When do you plan to do it?"

"I don't know. Pretty quick now."

"Saturday night."

"Not that soon."

"Yes that soon. We know all we have to know. This is Tuesday. I'll get us a car Friday. We've been over it enough. There's no use waiting any longer."

"I think so, too," Cannon said. "It's making me nervous."

He's right, Stone thought. They know I'm just stalling. Then he thought, Marianne, I'm sorry.

"All right," he said. "Saturday."

He listened to them talk. Guns and getaways, for God's sake, he thought. I can't do it, but I can't tell them. Or maybe I can't help but do it and I can't tell Marianne.

He had meant what he said to Marianne. But he meant what he said to Leeds and Cannon, too. He was going to do it, but he wasn't.

He knew Marianne was down in her trailer and he wanted to go to her, but he was afraid to.

Leeds left to go to work and Stone watched him through the window. He was walking rapidly and Stone thought he was probably whistling.

Jack Cannon said, "What's the matter, buddy?"

"Nothing. Just nerves."

"It's getting close. We've all got nerves."

"I guess." *Why can't I make up my mind? All I have to do is tell somebody something.* "I need some coffee," he said. "You're a hell of a maid."

He thought that what he would do probably was just drift along like this until Saturday night and then he still wouldn't know what to do so he would do whatever he had to.

I have to do something, he thought. Marianne. Oh God, Marianne, why did you have to love me?

Then he thought that was an odd way to look at it. The problem was not that he loved her, but that she loved him.

What in God's name am I going to do, he thought?

CHAPTER 15

Fran Novak looked in the screen door and said, "I want to talk to you."

Jack Cannon grinned. "Well, come on in and let's talk. I always like to talk."

She opened the door and stepped up into the trailer. Cannon was sitting on the couch, but she walked past him and looked down through the trailer. "Where are the others?" she said.

"Al's working. Burt went out somewhere. To a movie maybe. I don't know. Why?"

"I want to talk to you. It's important."

"All right. Go ahead."

"Marianne told me."

"Told you what?" he asked.

"You know what."

"No," he said. "How would I know what Marianne told you?"

"She told me about the robbery."

He grinned again. "Robbery? What's Marianne into now?"

"You know what robbery."

He stood up and went to the kitchen counter for a pack of cigarettes that was there. "No," he said, turning to look at her. "I don't know what robbery."

"The robbery that you're planning. You and Al and Burt."

"I sell insurance," he said, laughing. "I don't rob people."

He was surprised and he didn't know what to do. He was angry, but he knew how to handle his emotions. He smiled again and held out the pack of cigarettes. "Want one?" he said.

"No."

"All right."

"Jack," she said. "I know about it."

"Well, I don't. I don't know what you're talking about. You come in here and talk about a robbery that I'm planning—or have I done it already?"

"Not yet."

"Okay. A robbery I'm planning. And I'm supposed to know what you're talking about."

"Don't lie to me," she said. "You don't have to."

"I'm not lying. I really don't know anything about any robbery."

"Marianne told me."

"And where did Marianne find out?"

"From Burt. He was going to be in it, too, but she made him promise to get out."

"What?"

"He told her about it. Or rather, Sally did and then Marianne asked him about it. He promised to get out of it."

He laughed. "Hell," he said. "Someone's putting you on. There isn't any robbery."

She looked at him and said, "Jack, you don't have to tell me that. You don't have to lie to me."

"I'm not lying. If anyone's planning a robbery, I don't know anything about it." He grinned at her. "Besides, it must be all off if Burt's out of it."

"That's what he told Marianne."

"Then what are you worried about?"

"I'm worried about you."

"Me? I'm not about to get into a robbery. I like selling insurance."

He could tell by her expression that she was beginning to believe him.

"Don't lie to me," she repeated.

"I'm not lying. I really never heard of this before." He laughed again. "I don't think anyone else did either. Hell, if Burt and Al were planning something like that, I'd know about it." Then he said, "Did you say Burt *said* he wasn't going to do the robbery?" He thought: maybe Burt didn't make her understand.

"That's what he told Marianne. She was so upset about it, she made him promise not to do it."

"He told us this morning he was going to marry her."

"Really?"

"Sure. He said they decided last night."

"She didn't tell me that."

He sat down again on the couch. "Look," he said. "Let me talk to Al and Burt. If there's anything in all this, I can find out for you."

"You really aren't lying to me?" she said.

"Oh, hell," he answered, disgusted.

She got up and came to sit beside him. "Don't get angry," she said. "I just don't want you mixed up in anything."

"I'm not mixed up in anything," he said, imitating her voice. "You come in here with that wild story."

"It's true."

"I don't believe it. I'd know if anything like that was going on." He didn't have to pretend the anger that was in his voice. He thought: *Burt, you son of a bitch. What the hell are you doing? Maybe you're aiming to get everything and leave Al and me. You sure did get things fixed.*

"Don't get angry," she said. "I just didn't want you to get hurt."

"I'll get Marianne and get the facts about this thing," he said. He started for the door.

"Wait," she said. "Marianne didn't say you were in it. I don't think she did. I think we just assumed you were because Al and Burt are."

"Thanks a lot."

"Now wait," she said. "If you found out that Marianne and Sally were running a whorehouse down at the trailer, wouldn't you assume I was working at it, too."

She was defensive and that was what he wanted. "I guess I would," he said.

"Then don't get mad at me because I made the same assumption about you."

"I'm not working in a whorehouse. Not that I'd mind it." She laughed. "You're a nut," she said.

"Maybe, but I'm not a robber." He came back to the couch and sat down. "Hey," he said. "Who is it I'm supposed to rob?"

"The department store over at the shopping center."

"I wonder how much I'll get."

"Don't talk that way."

He put his arm around her and pulled her to him. He touched her breast and laughed. "I'd rather talk about this," he said.

"Are you really telling me the truth?"

"Yes."

"Promise me," she said.

He sat up straighter. "I said, yes. I'm telling you the truth."

"Don't get mad at me again." She took his hand and put it back on her breast. "I wouldn't want you to get mad at me."

"I'm not."

"Kiss me then."

He laughed and began to unbutton her blouse.

"Stop that," she said.

"I won't. Not unless you beg me to kiss you." He put his hand inside her brassiere. Her nipple was hard.

"Kiss me," she said.

"Beg."

"Please." She started to laugh, but he kissed her on the mouth. "It's the middle of the afternoon," she said then, "and I have things to do."

"I know you have."

"I don't mean that."

"Yes you do."

He kissed her again and when he tried to draw away, she held him and kissed him. Her mouth was open, that wild, sucking way she had when she kissed him.

"Let's go in the back," she said. "The door is open and people can see in."

He picked her up in his arms and her skirt fell away so that he held her thigh. Her skin was hot and he squeezed her leg and she put her face against his shoulder.

He carried her back through the trailer and she raised her face and kissed him while he walked. She made him want her even though he had started out at first only to make her believe what he was telling her.

But he was angry and confused, and it made him rough with her. He put her on the bed and he undressed her and then he lay down beside her and took her quickly, punishingly, but when she cried out at the end, he felt a wave of tenderness for her, and afterwards he held her gently and kissed her face.

"I didn't expect this when I came down here," she said once.

"I know."

"It's good when you don't expect it."

"Yes."

She turned over on her side and he could feel the tips of her naked breasts against his chest. It made his groin ache and he knew he wanted her again.

"Jack," she said. "You aren't lying to me, are you?"

"No."

She sighed and he pulled her tight against him and kissed her until she couldn't keep her hands or body still.

He lighted a cigarette and watched her walk toward her own trailer. She stumbled over one of the ridges in the street and looked back, grinning, and he waved at her.

When she was gone, he picked up the telephone book and looked up the number of the store where Al Leeds worked.

Leeds answered and said, "Who is it?"

"Cannon. We have a problem. Stone's putting us on."

There was a pause. "How?"

"Fran Novak was just down here. She was trying to talk me out of getting mixed up in the robbery."

"How'd she find out about it?"

"Marianne told her."

"What did you do?"

"I convinced her I didn't know about it, that it must be just you and Stone."

"What about Stone?"

"That's what I called to tell you. Stone's planning to back out. He didn't tell Marianne he'd marry her, he told her he wouldn't do the job." He waited, but Leeds didn't say anything. "We have to do something."

"I'll do something." Leeds paused again. "I thought you were Stone's buddy."

"I am, but we have to do something."

"Okay. I'll take care of it." Leeds hung up.

Cannon looked at the receiver. His hand was shaking. He was angrier than he had ever been in his life. He kept thinking, *what right did Stone have?* It surprised him. He hadn't really cared about the robbery. All he wanted to do was have some laughs and help Stone. But Stone didn't have any right to treat them that way.

Leeds waited for Stone at the bar.

He was there for half an hour before Stone arrived. He

sipped a beer and watched a ball game on television. But he was watching.

He saw Stone before he came in the door. He stood up and walked to the front to meet him.

"Hello, Burt," he said.

"What are you doing here?" Stone asked.

"Having a beer."

"You leaving now?"

"Are you trying to run me out?"

"No."

"I want to talk to you," Leeds said, his voice tight.

"Not now. I have to go to work." The other bartender was watching them.

"I want to talk to you now."

"So talk then."

"Outside."

Stone started to say something, but he turned abruptly and walked back outside. The bartender called to him, but Stone pretended that he hadn't heard. He went to the side of the building because it was quieter and darker there.

A truck went by on High Street and backfired. He glanced at it and then at Leeds. "All right, Al," he said. "What do you want?"

Leeds could feel his anger rising. "What do you think about Saturday night?" he said.

"We've been over that."

"Not over everything."

"I must have forgotten something that you just remembered," Stone said. His voice was hard, sarcastic.

"Yeah," Leeds said. "I just remembered something. Cannon isn't here."

"I know that."

"Cannon always gets between us, doesn't he?"

"He always has."

"And I just remembered something else. You know what it is."

"Do I?"

"You know you do, you son of a bitch. You know what's

wrong. You didn't fix anything with that broad. You're lying so hard you stink from it."

"All right," Stone admitted. "So I didn't fix it. I'm not going with you Saturday night. I'm out."

"No, you're not. You're still in."

Stone laughed. "What the hell can you do about it?" He laughed again. "You dumb bastard," he said.

Leeds hit him in the face. Stone went backwards and landed on his back. The blow landed high on his cheek and he could feel the cheekbone cut open, but he didn't touch the place.

He got up slowly, watching. Leeds moved toward him, but he swung a left that doubled Leeds over and then he followed with a right hand blow that landed on Leeds' ear and knocked him into the dirt.

"Stupid," Stone said. He kicked at Leeds and missed when Leeds rolled violently and jumped up.

They came together, swinging. Stone grabbed first and held, but Leeds brought a knee up, aiming for the groin, and Stone had to let go and step back.

Leeds swore and stepped in. Stone threw a punch straight and it caught Leeds moving forward and knocked him down again. The force shocked Stone's arm into the shoulder, but Leeds got up immediately. His mouth was bloody, but his eyes were clear.

Leeds feinted with a right and Stone ducked into a left hook that blacked him out, but when he came to he was hanging onto Leeds and punching at him. Leeds was grunting and trying to get free to have more room and Stone suddenly let go and slammed out with both hands and knocked him down again.

Leeds got to his knees, shaking his head. Stone skipped once, like approaching a football, and tried to kick Leeds in the face, but the latter reared back and caught Stone's foot and threw him. Stone landed on his shoulders, jarred, and he was only halfway to his feet when Leeds hit him twice. The second time smashed him down again and he tried to roll out of the way. Leeds kicked him in the side and he grunted in pain, but he still rolled and scrambled up.

They stood quiet for a moment, looking at each other, and Stone said, "I'll kill you."

Leeds didn't answer him. He waited and when Stone moved toward him, he jabbed twice, easy stabbing punches, and then he faked again with his right hand and Stone ducked. Leeds slashed with the left hook, but it glanced off Stone's shoulder before it landed, and it didn't do anything but sting. Stone cut back with a blow to the face that shook Leeds and made him groggy.

Leeds hooked the left again, this time to the body, and this time Stone wasn't ready for it and Leeds' fist sank into relaxed flesh and drove the breath out of it, and when Leeds hit him with his right hand, he didn't have any guard left and the punch landed flush.

It knocked Stone out, like an explosion in his head, but he didn't fall. He straightened, stiff, and Leeds hit him again, and then he fell and rolled onto his face in the cinders.

Leeds stood over him, panting. His hands hurt and his eye was cut. He spat out a mouthful of blood. "Now," he said. "Goddamn you. Get up."

Stone didn't move. He was spread-eagled on the ground and there was a gash on his cheek that Leeds could see

Leeds walked away and sagged against the side of the building. He had to spit out more blood and when he explored the inside of his mouth with his tongue, he found out that one of Stone's punches had torn open the inside of his cheek.

He was getting his breath back. He lit a cigarette and sucked hard on it. The smoke tasted sweet because of the blood and he held it in his lungs for a long time before he let it out.

Stone groaned and rolled onto his back. Leeds straightened up and walked over to him. "Get up," he said.

"Kiss my ass."

"Get up or I'll kick your teeth out."

Stone staggered when he was on his feet, but he caught himself.

"Now," Leeds said. "You're going to go through with it."

"You go to hell."

"You thought it was a good idea. You planned it."

"Now I'm going to forget it."

"I'll fight you again any time you want," Leeds said. "But first we're going to do this job."

"I told you."

"No. I'm telling you. This thing was all your idea, but no one is going to mess it up now. I'll see to it."

"You can kill me is all."

"No. I won't do that."

"There's nothing else you can do."

"Yes, there is."

"What?" Stone said. He touched his head. It hurt and he was dizzy.

"This Marianne. You must love her."

"Shut your mouth about her."

"You must love her. She's the one talked you out of everything."

"So what?"

"So I don't have to kill you."

Stone said, "If you touch her, I'll kill you."

"Maybe."

"No maybe."

"But if you don't stick with us until after Saturday night, you won't recognize her when I get finished."

Stone stepped toward him. But he was dizzy and he stopped.

"I won't do it," he said.

"Yes you will."

"You wouldn't hurt her."

"I will if I have to," Leeds said.

Stone looked at him and Leeds said, "I mean it. You know I mean it."

Stone touched his head again. A deep, sad resignation filled him. "All right," he said. "Leave her alone. I'll go with you Saturday night."

CHAPTER 16

Stone was alone in the trailer, lying on his bed, face down. His right hand was swollen and it hurt and his eye was closed, but his head didn't hurt any more now that he had slept some.

He wondered where Leeds and Cannon were. It didn't matter; he didn't care. He remembered dimly, just before he went to sleep, they were talking about one more run-through.

Someone knocked on the door. He didn't answer.

Marianne Nirvell called, "Burt?" When he didn't say anything, she said, "I know you're in there, Burt."

She came into the trailer. He didn't hear her until she was standing beside him. "The door was unlocked," she said. "Were you asleep?"

"No."

There was a lamp burning in the living room, but not much of the light came back, not enough to make him more than a dark shadow on the bed.

"I want to talk to you," she said.

"No. Leave me alone."

"You didn't tell them, did you?"

"No."

"Why not?"

"I don't know." His voice was dull and lifeless.

She caught her breath and leaned over him. "You're hurt," she said.

"No. I just fell down."

"I don't believe you."

He sat up and swung around to look at her. She started to say something when she saw his face, but he didn't give her a chance. "Leave me alone," he said. "I don't care whether you believe me or not."

"You can't do this. You said you loved me."

"Did I? Did you believe me?"

She turned away and said, "I don't believe you hurt

111

your face falling down. I think you fought with Al Leeds."

"If I did, I was beaten. So what difference does it make?"

She sat down beside him then and tried to put her arms around him, but he stood up and walked into the kitchen. She followed him.

"Burt," she said. "I know you love me. And I don't know why you're acting this way. But we can make everything all right if we try."

"No." he said. "No, we can't."

She seemed surprised and she said, "You know I love you. But I'll leave you if you do this. I won't ever see you again."

"Probably not."

"I won't tell anyone what you're doing, but I won't see you again."

"You said that."

"Burt, I love you." Her voice was a pained cry and her face looked drawn.

"I don't love you, though."

Her body shook as if she had just taken a chill, but when she spoke her voice was calm. "I don't believe that," she said.

He turned away from her and looked out the tiny kitchen window. "Go away from me," he said. "I don't want you, I don't need you. Just go away."

"You do need me."

He spun around. "Take a good look at my face. That's what you got me."

She went to him and put her arms around him and kissed him on the mouth. He started to kiss her back, but he jerked back and pushed her away.

"Leave me alone," he said.

"I don't care what you say. I know you love me. Is the money worth what it's costing you?"

"Yes, it's worth it."

"Look at me," she said. "I know what I look like." She cupped her breasts in her hands. "These are yours. How much money are they worth?"

"Stop it," he said.

"I won't stop it." She unbuttoned her blouse. He wanted

112

to look away, but she was tearing at her brassiere, trying to rip it open, and finally she flattened her breasts so she could pull the brassiere up. "You've kissed them," she said. "You've made love to me." She was beginning to cry and her voice had died to a whisper. "You held me while I was crying."

"Go away," he said.

He couldn't look away from her breasts. It wasn't erotic or obscene or funny or appealing or any of the other things that women usually are. It made her look vulnerable, off balance, out of focus, as if she had purposely made herself look ridiculous because she wanted to show him that she was giving him everything she could. The brassiere was still hooked and it was tight against the tops of her breasts, so that they were all out of shape. Weird. Like a Dali painting. He wanted to cover her. No woman should have to let a man gaze upon her when she looks like that.

"Make love to me, Burt," she said. "I need you."

"No." He was holding the edge of the sink, tight, and his hand throbbed. He thought about that, he held the pain in his mind so he wouldn't have to think about her. "Go away and leave me alone."

She walked to him and took his hand and tried to put it on her breast, but he pulled it away.

"Burt," she said.

He slapped her face.

She began to cry and he wanted to reach for her, to tell her how it really was. If she had stayed, he would have, but she turned and ran from the trailer, and it hit him that her breasts were still uncovered and he wanted to yell it after her. He went into the living room and looked out the window. She was running towards her own trailer, holding her blouse together, trying to cover herself, and he thought it was stupid that he would worry about anyone seeing her body.

He sat down on the couch and dug in his pocket for a cigarette. He was tired and his head had started to ache again.

The thing that bothered him most was losing the fight. He was ashamed of that. If he had won, things would be different. He could have made the rules and Leeds wouldn't have threatened to hurt Marianne.

He thought about the way Marianne's breasts looked, half uncovered that way, flattened out of shape by the pressure on them.

He knew Leeds meant what he said. Leeds would go after her.

"Goddamn it," he said out loud.

He stood up and went into the kitchen again. He opened the refrigerator and found a can of beer. He drank it, leaning on the counter. It tasted good and it helped him. It was cold; he wasn't so tired any more.

He went into the living room again and turned on the television set. He found a baseball game.

If I hadn't lost the fight, he thought. *I could be with Marianne right now. But I don't really have any reason to feel cheated. It was my idea. Leeds said it, but it's true. I was the one who started it.*

He couldn't forget the fight. His hand hurt and his headache was worse.

A car stopped in front of the trailer. Cannon and Leeds got out.

Stone took another swallow of beer and thought: *All right. If Saturday night has to be the night, then Saturday night will be the damnedest night of their lives.*

He grinned at them when they came in. "Where the hell have you been?" he said.

"We checked it out once more," Leeds said, watching him. "We're ready to go."

"So am I."

"Are you?" Cannon said.

"Oh come off it." Stone laughed. "So that chick gave me hot pants for a while. After that kick in the side Al gave me, I'm not going to get hot for anyone for a long time."

Cannon grinned, but Leeds looked suspicious. "So now you're all better," he said.

"I don't blame you guys for not trusting me, but things really are fixed now. Marianne was over here a little while

114

ago and I scared her a bit. She won't be talking to anyone."
He shrugged. "I don't seem to have a choice."

Leeds stared at him for a few seconds, but Stone looked
back at him and drank his beer.

CHAPTER 17

"What do you think?" Leeds said.

Cannon was driving slowly. "Think about what?"

"About Stone. Do you think he's telling the truth?"

"It's Saturday," Cannon said. "He's still with us."

"That doesn't mean he'll be there when we get back."

"I think he'll be there."

Leeds looked down a side street they were crossing. "He'd
better," he said.

"Or what'll you do?"

"He knows what I'll do."

Cannon glanced at him, but he didn't answer.

"Listen, man," Leeds said. "Don't waste any time getting
out there."

"I won't."

"Turn off anywhere in here."

Cannon turned into a side street. "Where?" he said.

"Keep driving. This is too close to people."

"Where are we going to find a car and no people?"

"I can jump a car in ten seconds."

"You've done this before?"

"No, man, not for real. But anybody knows how to jump
a car."

Cannon turned into another street. "How about this?"
he said. "Houses are far apart, but there's lots of cars."

"This is okay."

Canon slowed the car and stopped. Leeds opened the
door and got out. He stood, watching Cannon drive away,
then began to walk down the street.

He would have preferred to steal the car at night, but
it was summer and dark would be too late. If he had taken

it the previous night, he would have had to find a place to hide it.

He was tense and the palms of his hands were wet.

He found a black Buick that had unlocked doors. He stopped and glanced around, but he didn't see anyone. The lock button was up, but he tested the door handle. It worked easily.

He moved to the front of the car and swung open the hood. He already had the wires out of his pocket.

The engine roared and he looked up to see if anyone was coming, but no one was in sight, so he slammed the hood down, not caring now about noise, and he ran around the car and got into the driver's seat. The car had an automatic transmission. He would have liked a straight stick better, but he started smoothly and without tire noises. At the corner, he stopped and looked back. A man had turned into the block, but he wasn't looking for a car.

Leeds grinned tightly and drove away.

He was excited, but he made himself keep the speed down, and once he passed a police cruiser, but there hadn't been time enough for an alarm, so he didn't worry about that. The traffic was light and he made good time and still didn't have to worry about breaking any traffic laws.

By the time he left Westerville, he was relaxed and he lit a cigarette and fiddled with the radio. It was a good car and whoever owned it had taken care of it. It wasn't new—he had purposely picked one that wouldn't attract notice—but it handled well and the engine was good.

He increased his speed.

He found the side road that he and Cannon had agreed on and he slowed to make the turn.

Cannon had parked his car and was standing beside it, waiting. Leeds pulled up and he got in. "Didn't take you long," he said.

"I told you it wouldn't."

"You get a good one?"

Leeds nodded. He turned the car around and started back to the highway. "You leave your car unlocked?"

"Yes."

"Good. I don't want to have to waste any more time than necessary switching cars."

Cannon stretched his legs in front of him. "I'm getting jumpy," he said.

"So am I."

"We'll make it."

Leeds looked at him, his eyes suddenly narrow and hard. "I wasn't saying I wanted to quit."

"Neither was I."

They passed the Westerville limits. "If we don't get picked up first," Leeds said, "I wonder how long we'll have before someone calls the car in stolen."

"Long enough."

"Yeah." He was surprised at his nerves. That damned Stone was the one thing that was worrying him.

"Turn here," Cannon said. "We'll meet less traffic."

Leeds nodded and swung the car left. Heavy clouds had blown up in the sky and it looked as if it would rain soon. But the sun was shining and it made the sky a burned color, nearly gray, but still yellow—like burned milk.

Cannon lit a cigarette.

"Give me one," Leeds said. He took the pack and shook one out. He used the lighter on the dashboard.

"What are you going to do after it's over?" Cannon queried.

"Ask me tomorrow."

Cannon looked up at the sky. "I hope Burt has the guns ready," he said. "We're running short on time."

"Yeah."

Cannon laughed. "You really do sound jumpy."

"I don't trust Stone."

"He's with us."

"Yeah? And what are we going to do if he's taken off?"

"Wait for him."

"In a stolen car?"

"I don't know," Cannon said. "He'll be there."

"He'd better be."

117

"Why don't you shut up about it? You're making me nervous, too."

When they were a block from the trailer park, Leeds said, "We'd better park here."

A breeze had come up. It made dust swirls in the gutter, but it dried the sweat on Leeds' face.

"I don't see him," he said when they got to the trailer.

"He's probably in the back or something."

Stone was on the couch, waiting. Leeds stepped into the trailer and stopped. Stone was pointing a gun at him.

"Come in," Stone said. "I've been waiting for you."

Cannon came in behind Leeds. "You ready?" he said.

Stone stood up and walked toward Leeds. "I'm ready," he said. He handed the gun to him. "The clips are on the table," he added.

"Goddamn you," Leeds said.

"What's the matter now?" Cannon asked.

"Nothing."

"What are you swearing for?"

Stone turned and walked back to the couch. "He's nervous. Here's yours." He threw a gun to Cannon.

"Take it easy."

"It's not loaded yet. Where's the car?"

"A little way from here. We'll walk to it."

Leeds was still by the door, holding the gun. Stone said, "The clips are on the table there, Al. Get loaded up."

Leeds looked at him for a moment more, but when Stone straightened up to face him, he turned and went to the table. He picked up a clip of shells and put it into the butt of the automatic.

"Come on," Stone said. "Let's get going."

Cannon loaded his gun. "Where's yours?"

"Stuck in my belt under my shirt."

"Just like Jesse James," Leeds said.

Stone ignored him. "Let's go. You guys were so anxious, let's get going."

Leeds looked at his watch. "Eight-twenty."

"The timing's right so far," Stone said. "But it'll take us twenty-five minutes to get there."

"All right." Cannon went out first.

Stone and Cannon got into the car while Leeds used the jump wire to start it again. When Leeds got in, he looked at Stone in the back seat and said, "I didn't think you'd be there when we got back."

"I said I would be, didn't I?"

"Come on," Cannon said. "You guys can argue later. Let's go."

"You get the other car placed?" Stone said.

"We took care of it."

"Well, keep the motor hot on this one while Jack and I are in the store." He laughed.

"What's the matter?" Cannon said.

"I was just thinking what a mess we'd be in if we came storming out and old Al here killed the engine and had to get out and open the hood to start it again."

"Don't sweat over that," Leeds said. He turned the car into another street and looked in the rearview mirror. Stone was leaning against the side of the car, one leg on the seat.

The sun was completely covered by clouds now, but they had lightened and it didn't look so much like rain.

They drove in silence and after a few more minutes, Cannon said, "There's High Street. Almost there."

"I can see the entrance sign," Leeds said.

"What's Sally doing there tonight?" Stone said.

"She's in the office, but she'll be out by the time we hit it."

"Fine. I'm glad to see you thought of everything."

Leeds looked in the mirror again. Stone hadn't moved, but he was grinning widely. "What's the matter with you?" he said.

"Nothing," Stone said. "Why? Does it make you nervous to have me behind you?"

"No." He could see the entrance to the shopping center. "It should."

Leeds turned to look. Stone was sitting up straight. He had a gun in his hand. He grinned at Leeds and said, "Keep both your hands on the wheel where I can see them."

"What the hell's going on?" Cannon said.

Stone didn't look at him. "You just keep driving straight ahead, Al."

"What if I don't?"

Stone leaned forward and laid the gun's barrel against Leeds' neck. "I think you'd better," he said.

"I'll kill you."

"No, I'll kill you."

Cannon said, "Burt, what the hell are you doing?"

Stone didn't look away from Leeds. "We're not robbing any store tonight, Jack. This stupid bastard thought he could make me do it, but he's finding out now."

Cannon started to reach for him. Leeds tensed, but he didn't turn his head when Stone said, "Jack, if you touch me, I'll blow his head off. I swear to God I will. And you saw the hole a forty-five makes." Then he laughed and said, "Why don't you say something, Al? You were talkative as hell the night you told me what you were going to do to Marianne."

"You have the gun."

"You have one, too."

"I haven't forgotten it."

"Jack, you reach over there and take it out of Al's belt and then hand it to me. Easy."

He took it and dropped it on the floor. "Now, Al," he said, "pull up at the next corner and stop."

"What are you going to do?" Cannon asked.

"Stop at the corner, Al."

Leeds didn't say anything. There was a nervous tic showing in his jaw. He drove to the curb and stopped.

"Get out, Jack," Stone said.

"What?"

"Get out. This is between Al and me and I don't want to have to watch you."

Cannon opened the door, but he didn't get out until Stone said, "Get out or I'll kill him right now."

"He means it," Leeds said, his face white and strained. "Get out."

"What are you going to do?" Cannon said. He was out, but he hadn't shut the door.

"It doesn't have anything to do with you," Stone said.

He looked at Cannon for the first time since drawing the gun. "Close the door. Now."

Cannon stood on the sidewalk and watched them drive away.

"What do we do now?" Leeds said.

"Just keep driving South on High Street. I'll tell you where to go."

"What's this going to get you?"

"Satisfaction."

"If you kill me, you're in for more trouble than just robbery."

"It's a different kind of trouble. If I kill you."

They stopped for a red light. Leeds reached for a cigarette and Stone jabbed him with the gun. "Keep your hands in sight," he said.

"I just want a cigarette."

"Nervous?"

"Yes, I'm nervous."

"I thought you would be."

Leeds started to turn his head to look back, but the gun dug into his neck and he stopped.

"The light's green," Stone said. "Go on."

"What if I just sit here?" Someone blew a horn.

"I don't think you'd better."

"You wouldn't kill me here."

"You'd better not bet on it."

Leeds hesitated, but the horn blew again, and he drove across the intersection. "I'm not afraid of you," he said.

"I didn't expect you to be."

The sun was setting. It had come from behind the clouds and had turned them red.

"Where are we going?" Leeds said.

"You remember the stone quarry where we went swimming when we first came to Columbus?"

"Yes."

"Drive there." Stone shifted his weight and the gun moved back from Leeds' neck. "And I remember the way," he said.

Leeds turned right and looked in the mirror. Stone was sitting on the edge of the seat, but he had his feet spread and he had a firm hold on the gun. There was no chance of a sudden turn throwing him across the seat.

"What do we do when we get there?" eLeds asked.

"You'll find out when we're there."

"You wouldn't shoot me without giving me a chance."

Stone laughed out loud. "Hell yes, I would," he said. "If you're going to shoot a man, the time to do it is when he's unarmed."

"Thanks," Leeds said. "I'd do the same for you."

"I know you would."

"Why did we ever become buddies?"

"I don't know." Stone gestured curtly. "You turn right up there ahead."

Leeds looked in the mirror again. He was surprised that he wasn't afraid. He was going to put up a fight if he had any chance at all, but he expected to die. Only fools attack a gun when they're unarmed and expect to survive. He thought he was going to die. It was a real feeling. He thought: *Another ten minutes, fifteen, I'm going to be dead.*

He could almost picture what his dead body would look like and he couldn't understand why he wasn't scared. He was so tense that his arms were beginning to cramp, but he wasn't frightened, and in a way, that disappointed him. What the hell kind of life is it that you're not afraid to lose?

He saw the turnoff and he was going to drive past it, just to try, but Stone poked him with the gun and said, "There. Turn in."

He made the turn and he had to slow down to ten miles an hour because the lane was rutted and narrow.

It was darker off the highway. It was deep dusk, but in the open there was light yet. Here, he could barely see to drive. He mentioned that to Stone.

"No lights," Stone said. His voice was higher, now, not so casual, and he was leaning forward more. But he hadn't moved the gun away.

Leeds stopped the car. "This is as far as we can go."

Stone peered ahead. "Why?"

"It drops off to the water. You can't see it; it's too dark, but it drops off."

"Okay," Stone grunted. "Get out."

"Maybe I'd just as soon have it here."

"Get out."

He wanted to get out, he couldn't move in the car, but he didn't want to look too eager.

"Wait," Stone said. He got out the back and stood away from the front door. "Now."

Leeds swung out and onto his feet. He started forward, but Stone stepped aside and said, "Don't," and he stopped.

Leeds caught himself tightening his stomach muscles, as if he could stop the bullet that way if it just didn't take him by surprise.

CHAPTER 18

Fran Novak and Marianne Nirvell had been waiting. When Jack Cannon parked his car in front of the trailer, they ran toward him.

"What's happened?" Marianne said. She wasn't wearing makeup and she had been crying.

"I don't know," he said. He walked past them and went into the trailer, but they followed him.

"What happened, Jack?" Fran said.

"Did you do the robbery?" Marianne said.

"No, we didn't do any goddamn robbery," Cannon said, mimicking her tone. He swung around, angry, and then he turned back when he saw her face and went to the kitchen. He opened the refrigerator and took out a can of beer.

Marianne took him by the arm and tried to turn him. "You have to tell us," she said.

"Stone backed out at the last minute."

"What did he do?"

"Nothing, damn it. He didn't do a thing. Leave me alone. I wish to God I'd never heard of either one of them." He shoved her aside and opened a drawer to look for a can opener. But then he straightened up and looked at Marianne. "I'm sorry," he said. "It's not your fault. Just everything got all screwed up. It was a dumb thing to start with."

Fran said, "You were in it, and you were lying to me."

"Yes, I was lying to you."

"I believed you at first."

"Sure you did. That's why I make a good insurance salesman."

Marianne took his arm again. "Where's Burt now?"

"I don't know."

"What do you mean you don't know? Where's Al?"

"With Burt, wherever that is."

"My God!" Marianne said. "What are they going to do?"

"I don't know." He began looking for the can opener again.

"You have to tell me what happened," Marianne said. He wouldn't look at her and she held his arm and tried to pull him. "Tell me."

He found the can opener and punched holes in the beer can. He took a long swallow. Then he said, "Burt pulled a gun and held it on Al. He made me get out of the car. Then they drove away. My car was parked out where we were going to switch from the one Al swiped. I took a cab out after it and I came back here. That's all I know."

"Oh my God!" Marianne said. Her eyes were wide with shock and worry.

"What did Al do?" Fran asked hollowly.

Cannon laughed harshly. "You don't do much of anything with a forty-five stuck in the back of your neck."

"What are we going to do?" Marianne said.

"We can call the police."

"No," Cannon said. "Don't call the cops. They're in a stolen car and they're carrying illegal weapons." He remembered his own gun and he lifted his shirt and pulled it out of his belt. He laid it on the counter. "If you care anything about either one of them, don't call the cops."

"They may kill each other," Marianne said.

Cannon looked at her bleakly. "You mean you're afraid Burt might get hurt."

"But I don't want Burt to kill anyone either," she cried.

"Well, Burt has the guns and I don't know where they

are so I don't see how we can do anything about it either way."

"Jack," Fran said, "we should call the police."

"Go ahead then. I'm out of it. You can go visit them on Sundays. Or whenever." He looked out the window. "Oh hell," he said. "I like them both."

"What are you going to do with that gun?"

"I'd better get rid of it."

"I'll hide it for you at our place. If the police come here, they won't have any reason to search our trailer."

"Take the damn thing. I'll be glad to have it out of here," Cannon said.

"I'll call the police, too."

"No," Marianne said. "No. They'll find Burt."

"You want him to kill someone?"

"He won't kill anyone."

"Get that gun out of here," Cannon ordered.

Fran was looking at Marianne. "All right," she said. "I won't call the police. I think I should, but I won't."

She picked up the gun and went out. Cannon walked to the window to watch her go. When he turned back, Marianne was standing by the sink. She was pale, but she wasn't crying, and he felt a sympathy for her.

"It'll work out," he said. She looked at him and didn't answer and he said, "You said yourself that Burt isn't the kind to kill anyone. So why worry?"

"Why did he do it?" she said. "He promised me he wouldn't."

"He and Leeds had a big fight over it and Leeds won."

"But he couldn't force Burt to do anything."

"He had a lever."

"A lever? What lever?"

"You. He said he'd come after you if Burt tried to back out. Burt was afraid Leeds would try to take it out on you. That's why he said he'd go along with us. Leeds said he'd get you if he didn't."

Marianne nodded and looked past him, out the curved front window of the trailer, but all she could see was them, reflected on the darkened glass. "What do you think Burt will do?" she said.

"I don't know."

"I think he may kill Leeds."

"You changed your mind fast."

"He might kill him because he loves me."

That was such an unexpected thing to say that it made Cannon want to laugh, but he looked at her and he understood her and he was afraid she might be right.

Fran came back into the trailer. She had Sally with her. Sally was frightened, but she was trying not to show it.

"I hid the gun," Fran said.

"What's happened?" Sally said. "She won't tell me."

"I told her all we know," Fran said.

"That's it," Cannon said. "We don't know anything else."

"You're lying to me."

"Shut up," Marianne said suddenly. "We don't know anything either."

"I came home and I was waiting," Sally said to Cannon. "Just like Al told me to."

"Nothing else went the way Al said," Cannon muttered.

Marianne went to the door and stared out. "I have to do something."

Fran went to her and put her arms around her. "There isn't anything to do," she said.

"We can go look for them." She spun around to look at Cannon. "You know them. Where would they go?"

"I don't know. We never killed each other before."

"Jack," Fran said.

"Well, Jesus Christ, I'm worried, too. But I don't know where they are and I don't know where we could look."

"Well, we can't just stay here and wait," Marianne said. Her voice rose. "I can't stand it to just wait here."

"There's nothing else to do."

"There has to be something."

"No," Cannon said. "We'll just wait."

Marianne said, "Not here. I'm going home."

Fran said, "Why?"

"He'll call me there, of course. Burt will call me there."

"She's right," Cannon said. "Burt would call her."

Sally laughed suddenly. "Or Al," she said. "Burt may

have had the guns when you saw them last, but it still might be Al who calls. For me."

Leeds could hear the crickets.

They were all around him, loud, and he listened to them because there wasn't much else he could do. He wasn't afraid and Stone wouldn't get within reach, so there wasn't anything he could do.

"What's it going to be?" he said.

Stone motioned with the gun. "Get away from the car."

"Why? You afraid you'll ruin the paint job."

"Maybe."

"A little blood won't matter on black."

"Move away from the car."

Leeds edged sideways. "You're not going to get anything out of this."

"Take off your clothes."

"Why, man? You have a thing about shooting naked people?"

"I'm not going to kill you. But I will if I have to."

"I'll try not to do anything rash then."

"Take off your clothes," Stone repeated impatiently.

"I said, why?"

"Because it'll take you longer to get back to town naked. I want time."

"Time to run?"

"Yes."

"You'll need it."

"I don't think you'll come after us."

Leeds laughed nastily. "Us? You and that broad."

"Take off your clothes."

Leeds began to unbutton his shirt. A screech owl hooted and he stopped, startled. It was open around the quarry, but the clouds had closed in tight and it was dark.

"I'll find you," he said.

"That could make me kill you." Stone stepped closer. "Hurry up," he said. He looked up at the sky.

Without warning, Leeds hurled himself at Stone's legs and they went down together. He heard the gun hit rock when Stone dropped it and he rolled free and scrambled for it, but Stone jumped on him and grabbed him around the neck.

He wanted to hurt Stone. *Doublecrossing, damned superior Stone.* That's why he jumped him when all he had to do was wait. He was afraid Stone would get away and he wouldn't be able to find him.

He was strangling. He tried to yell but he couldn't. He slammed his head back, hard, and it hit Stone in the face and broke the hold.

Leeds rolled over and moved to get his feet, but Stone was up first and he swung a vicious right-hand uppercut that smashed Leeds over backwards.

His head hit something hard and he thought it was a rock and he grabbed for it. He was going to throw it; Stone was coming toward him. But it was the gun. He yelled and brought it over his head and fired.

It shocked him the way the bullet slammed Stone back. It looked as if he had been hit by a truck. He didn't fall, he was thrown back to the ground.

Leeds didn't move at first. He just held the gun and looked across at Stone. Then he shuddered and threw the gun away from him. He got up and walked over to Stone and looked down and said, "Jesus Christ, Burt."

All the anger and resentment had drained out of him and he felt scared now, cheated, because it wasn't supposed to happen this way. It was one thing to face your own death! It was something else to look at another man's and be responsible for it!

Leeds ran to the car and got in. He was fumbling for keys before he remembered and he got out again and opened the hood. His hands were shaking; he had trouble starting the engine. Then he remembered the gun and he had to stop and think about the direction in which he had thrown it.

He couldn't find it. He crawled around on his hands and knees, looking for it, but to no avail. He swore savagely because if he hadn't he would have cried.

His hand finally struck the gun and he sobbed in his throat in his relief. Picking it up, he got to his feet and looked at it. He thought it still felt hot.

He ran to the edge of the water and threw the weapon as far out as he could and he didn't move until he heard the splash.

Turning, he looked over at Stone again before he ran for the car. He didn't switch on the lights, but he drove as fast as he could.

Stone didn't know what had happened to him. He remembered being hit harder than anything had ever hit him and that was all.

He tried to sit up and the pain struck him so badly he cried out.

"Goddamn Leeds," he moaned.

He tried a second time to rise, but he fell forward on his face and had to lie there, resting, until he had strength enough to try it again. Then he staggered, but he was able to stay up.

He hurt. The pain was sharp, hot, and it made him want to yell, but he bit down on his lip and tried to see how bad it was. Now he remembered the explosion, the gun, and he knew he had been shot, but he didn't know where. The whole upper half of his body was burning and he had to poke around with the fingers of his left hand until he found the wound.

The bullet had cut into his right shoulder, close to his neck, but it left a furrow and not a hole. He was bleeding, but not too badly, and he knew the bullet had gone on and wasn't in him somewhere.

He had to sit down to rest. He was sweating hard and he thought maybe he was going into shock. He was losing some blood, but it wouldn't be too bad if he could get medical attention.

Only he couldn't go to a hospital. Gunshot wounds get reported to the police.

He struggled up again and began to walk. The bleeding was slow, but it was running down his body, inside his shirt.

Every step made him shudder. But the further he went, the less it hurt. It was numbing. His mind was clear, though he didn't know how long that would last. He had to keep thinking of something besides the pain. If he could do that, he might avoid shock.

He stumbled onto the highway and stood still. A car went by and he waved, but it didn't stop.

The next car slowed, but it went faster again, and he wondered just how bedraggled he must look. Maybe no one would pick him up. What then, oh great white warrior? God, it hurt.

A truck stopped beside him and a thin, Negro voice, dialect, said, "Whatsa matter, buddy?"

"I need a ride."

"You all right?"

"I just want a ride."

He heard an emergency brake being pulled and a man got out and came around to him. "You sick?" the man said. He put an arm under Stone's armpit to support him, but he pulled it away immediately and looked at his hand. "You been cut?" he said.

"No. I just need a ride."

"You needs a hospital more."

"No."

The man took hold of him again to support him. "Whatever you say," he said. "Come on. Let's get you in the truck." He helped him in, then came around to the other side and climbed in beside him. "Who cut you?" he said.

"Nobody."

"You didn't do that by your lonesome."

Stone looked at him. "I got shot," he said.

"You needs a hospital, man," the Negro said. "Bullets ain't to fool with."

"I can't go to a hospital."

"You hot?"

"I will be in the hospital, but nobody's chasing me."

"How 'bout the man shot you?"

"He must think he killed me."

"Yeah, man," the Negro said.

Stone put his head on the back of the seat. "I'm bleeding on your seat," he said, beginning to laugh.

"How bad you shot?"

"Not bad. Bullet went on. It's not in me."

"I got shot once."

"Did it kill you?"

The Negro looked at him sharply. "You got someone to take care of you?"

"Marianne. Marianne, the nurse."

"You better tell me where your Marianne is. I got a feeling you're going to leave me."

"I'll stay awake."

"Where, man?"

"Trailer park. Westerville Road. Fifty-seven twenty. Lot twenty-six." He looked at the Negro. "Don't you take me to the cops," he said.

"I'll get you there," the Negro said. "But I sure do hope you know what you're saying. I don't want you dying on me."

"Marianne, the nurse. Don't forget that."

He was talking as if he were drunk. If it didn't hurt so, I'd feel drunk, he thought. I have to stay awake. This guy's too much good luck.

"Hurry up," he said.

"Going as fast as I can now."

He touched his shoulder. The blood was beginning to dry. It wasn't bad. He was tired and weak and he hurt and he wasn't completely clear any more.

CHAPTER 19

Leeds stopped the car in front of the store. Most of the lights inside had been turned off, but he could still see some lit in the back.

He got out and walked to the door. He rattled it, but it was locked. He tried again, shaking the door hard, and waited, but still no one came to see what he wanted.

He stepped back and looked up and down the street. About twenty feet away, there was an outdoor telephone booth. He looked back into the store, but he couldn't see anyone.

He was tight, nervous, but he felt mean, as if he wanted

to hurt someone. He felt cheated, as if he had been shoved into something, as if he had been manipulated and used, and now was about to be crushed because he wasn't useful any more.

To hell with that.

The gun was in his pocket. He could feel it there, heavy and cold. He had nearly forgotten about it and he had been halfway back into town before he remembered that Stone had dropped it on the floor in the back of the car.

He walked to the telephone booth.

There wasn't any book and he had to call information to get the number of the store, but he got it.

A man answered and Leeds said, "Listen, I know you're closed, but this is kind of an emergency. I wonder if you can help me."

"What is it?' the man asked.

"I need a white dress shirt. Something came up and I have to have a shirt and all mine are in the laundry. I drove over here and I saw your lights on in the back. I was wondering if you could let me in and sell me one."

The man laughed. "Well, we can't let a customer down in an emergency. Where are you now?"

"I'm in the phone booth just outside."

"I'll come up then."

"Thank you very much," Leeds said. "I'll be there."

He hung up and walked back to the store.

The manager was a heavy man, about fifty years of age—a handsome man with gray hair. He smiled when he unlocked the door and then he said, "I'll bet there's a girl involved. Nothing else could make you so desperate for a new shirt."

"Sure," Leeds said. "You guessed it right." He stepped inside and turned around to see if there was anyone driving by outside.

"What kind of shirt did you have in mind?" the manager inquired.

Leeds took the gun out of his pocket. "Let's go back to the office."

He was nervous and he didn't like the manager.

The manager's keys were still hanging in the front door and he let himself out.

"All right," the manager said nervously, his lips trembling. "Take it easy with that thing."

"Let's go."

"Take it easy. I'm not going to fight you for insured money."

"Good for you," Leeds said. He pointed the gun. "Let's go, I said."

The man turned around and walked toward the office. He kept looking over his shoulder at Leeds. They went into the office and the manager stood beside a desk, leaning against it.

"Get out the money," Leeds ordered.

"It's in that bag, on the other desk."

Leeds pointed to the safe. "How about in there?"

"Only a few hundred to open up with Monday morning."

"Open it."

"If I do, it sets off an alarm. Once it's closed for the night, it can't be opened until morning without setting off an alarm."

Leeds walked to the safe and looked at it. "Sure," he said. "And you're so worried about me, you tell me all about it."

The manager shrugged. "I open that thing and a bell starts ringing. So you get excited and shoot me. That's what I'm worried about."

Leeds turned to look at the safe again. At that precise instant the manager jumped at him and caught him around the neck from behind. They fell against the safe and Leeds dropped the gun, but he twisted sideways and broke the manager's hold on him. When the latter tried to grab him again, Leeds hit him twice in the face and knocked him down.

Leeds bent to scoop up the gun. When he stood up, the manager was on his knees, shaking his head, and Leeds hit him in the temple with the butt end of the gun.

The man flattened out on the floor and lay still. Leeds grabbed the money bag without looking at him and ran out of the office.

He felt excited now, like just before a race, and he thought: *It doesn't make any difference any more. Stone's dead. Maybe that guy back there is dead, too! I hit him pretty hard. So what the hell? You take some chances and you come out ahead every time.*

Climbing into the car, he stuffed the money back under the front seat.

He wanted to rush out of there, but he forced himself to drive away slowly, and he stopped and looked both ways before he left the parking lot and drove onto the highway.

He felt like laughing. All the plans, the waiting, and he just walked up there and took the money all by himself!

But there was a tight knot of fear in his belly and he knew that's why he wanted to laugh. He thought about Stone, lying back there by the water. He hadn't planned it that way.

Stone's fault, he thought. *He was the one who messed himself up.*

A siren started up behind him. He looked in the rear view mirror and he saw a patrol car coming fast in the outside lane.

Easy, he thought. *Maybe they're not after me. Maybe they're going to a fire or an accident.*

But he was driving a stolen car and he had stolen money in it and he had killed at least one man, maybe two.

He slammed down on the accelerator and the car shifted into passing gear and jumped ahead. He looked back again and the patrol car had dropped back.

He went through Worthington at sixty-five and he almost was stopped when a car passed in front of him at an intersection, but he rammed on through the red light and kept going. The car he almost hit stopped and that slowed the cruiser some, but it shook loose and the siren stayed with him.

He was on the highway now and he had the Buick open as much as it would go. The speedometer read one hundred twenty, but he knew it wasn't going that fast. Maybe a hundred miles an hour.

The patrol car had dropped back still further, but it hadn't given up the case.

134

Leeds really wanted to laugh now. He was yelling, calling to the police, and he knew he was acting silly, but he couldn't help it. It was fun this way. There was a great bursting sensation in his chest, an exuberant feeling that he couldn't shake off, and it made him want to laugh at being chased.

He passed a car and caught a glimpse of a woman's face. She looked frightened.

The patrol car was gaining now he suddenly noticed. He had the Buick full out, but the cruiser was souped up and it was steadily drawing closer. But he had maybe a seven hundred yard lead, and he knew how to drive.

There was a sharp curve and he hit it fast and skidded into the left lane. He spun the wheel skillfully and rocked the car to the right without touching the brake. When he looked back that time, the patrol car had slowed to make the curve and had lost ground.

God, it felt good to run. Sometimes a man has to get out and run. He was laughing hard now, leaning over the wheel, and he could no longer hear the siren.

He crossed the top of a hill and dropped down to the other side of it and for a few seconds he was alone. There wasn't anything in his mirror, and it made him feel like maybe he had it made. He laughed, but the cruiser's lights picked him up again and for a moment he shivered, afraid.

There was something about that patrol car, not the police officers in it, but the car itself. It was like a bloodhound. It wouldn't quit, wouldn't go away. He couldn't win because there wasn't any finish line. He had the Buick sprung clear out, but the cruiser wouldn't go away.

Maybe his whole life had been like that, maybe something had been chasing him all the time.

The hell with it! He could still run, he could still drive better than any cop, and he still had a bag full of money under the seat.

Just get away. Get away and all the money was his. Shake the cruiser for a few minutes and he could get rid of the car. He could run with the money, and they wouldn't ever catch him.

But he had to get away from that cruiser first.

A car was stopped at an intersection, its lights blinking for a left turn, and he went sliding around on the other side. His tires hit gravel and the Buick's rear end whipped hard, but he rode it and came out on the other side without slowing down.

The Buick's motor was whining and screaming, but he couldn't get any more out of it.

He passed four cars at once, shot past them all, and it made him grin to think of what the people in them would be saying.

"That damn fool's going to kill himself," they would say.

And he would answer, "So what? There's worse things than dying. Everybody dies. What's important is, you live first. If you do that, it doesn't matter how old you are when you die. Right?"

That's what he'd say.

He heard an odd sound, like caps going off in some kid's gun, and then he thought: *They're shooting at me!*

Funny, it didn't scare him. He thought it was funny. One hundred miles an hour and they were shooting at him.

He slammed into another curve and when he came out, the police had dropped further back and were too far away to shoot.

Leeds crouched closer over the wheel, as if leaning forward would make the Buick go faster. Ahead of him there was a long hill and he climbed into it, nursing the car's speed.

The hill was clear. He hit the crest without losing much speed. He was doing eighty and he glanced back to see where the cops were. They were nearly a mile back; he could still see the blinking red light, but he had outrun the siren.

He saw the truck coming then and there was nothing he could do to miss it. The road was cut down into the hill and on either side of it was a wall of rock. The truck was in his lane, a furniture van that was trying to pass a flat bed truck with steel on it.

He had time to yell, "No," and then he crashed into the front of the truck.

His tremendous speed and the impact of the crash drove

136

the engine back through the car, crushing him, but for some reason the car didn't burn.

He didn't feel any pain. He just yelled that one word and then everything exploded into light and that was all.

When the police got there, he was still in the car, but they found the bag of money in a ditch.

CHAPTER 20

The Negro stopped the truck. "This the place?" he said.

"Red. Red Trailer."

"Can you make it?"

"No."

"You want me to go in there."

"They'll help you get me out."

"You sure, man?"

"Yes."

But Cannon was already out of the trailer. "Who's there?" he said.

"That's Jack," Stone said. "Tell him it's Burt."

"Burt," the Negro said. "I got your Burt in here."

Cannon came around and opened the door. "What's wrong?"

Stone giggled. "I seem to have been shot," he said. He eased himself out and Cannon caught him.

The Negro was still in the truck.

"Money," Stone said. "Give him the money that's in my wallet."

The girls had come out and Fran and Marianne helped him inside. Cannon gave the Negro forty dollars. The man nodded and looked curiously at the trailer, but he didn't say anything. He put the truck in gear and drove away.

Stone was in the back, on Marianne's bed. She had ripped his shirt open and she was looking at the wound.

"He needs a doctor," Cannon said.

"No cops," Stone said.

"Where's Al?" Sally said from the doorway. "I told you Al wouldn't get killed."

Stone looked up at her. "I don't know where he is," he said. "But he didn't get shot." He laughed.

Marianne went to a built-in dresser and took out a bottle of alcohol. She brought it back and bent over him. Then she stooped and kissed him. "You need a doctor," she said.

"No doctor. You."

"You should be in a hospital. I'm not a doctor."

"I am." He laughed again. "It's not bad, nurse. Just a flesh wound. No bullet in the hole. Song title. No bullet in the wound." He winced and said, "Please, Marianne." His voice cracked with the pain.

"All right," she said, frowning, tears immobilized in her eyes, her lower lip trembling just a little. "I'll take care of it."

She gave him a piece of sheeting, folded into a small pad, and she told him to bite on it while she cleaned the wound. She said it would keep him from screaming.

Cannon took Fran Novak by the arm and drew her out of the room. Sally was leaning against the wall, watching.

Cannon said, "Leeds will come back here."

"Why would he?"

"He probably thinks Burt is dead and he's going to want to run, but he'll need money and he's got nearly seven hundred dollars over there from that race money. He'll come after it."

"Should we call the police?" Fran queried.

"No. Not now." He scratched his head. "I don't know what to do," he said.

"I think we should call the police."

"They'll take Burt."

"What can they charge with him?"

"I don't know, but they'd think of something." He pulled her to the window. "Listen, keep an eye on the street here. If Al comes here, you'll see the car. Watch for it."

"What are you going to do?" Fran asked nervously.

"See if I can help with Burt."

"I mean when Al comes."

"I don't know," he said. "Maybe I'll get shot, too."

He walked to the back. Stone was sitting on the edge

of the bed, holding the piece of sheeting in his hand, but his lips were white and he was sweating.

"How's it coming, buddy?" Cannon said.

Stone nodded. Then with an effort he grinned and said, "I thought you might shoot me, too."

"Hell," Cannon said. "I didn't really want to be a robber anyway. I really wanted to be a cowboy."

Stone tried to grin at him again, but Sally Talent said, "You dirty bastards. Both of you let Al down flat, didn't you?"

Stone looked at her and then at Cannon, but neither of them answered her.

Marianne said, "Almost done." She began to wind bandage around his shoulder.

"Get me a shirt, Jack," Stone said.

Cannon took off his and handed it to him. He still wore a white tee shirt. "I don't want to go down there now," he said. "I've got Fran watching for Al."

"You think he'll come here."

"He's got that money down there."

"I forgot that."

"You should have blood," Marianne said.

"You have any to spare?"

"You'll have to rest instead."

She began to cry and he stared at her, startled, but she put her head in his lap and all he could do was stroke her hair.

Sally walked out of the room. She brushed past Cannon and said, "I still think Al will come after me."

"Maybe," Cannon said. He followed her to the front of the trailer.

Marianne said, "I was so worried about you."

"After the way I treated you?"

"Jack told me what Al did to you."

"He whipped hell out of me."

"I mean, what he said he'd do to me."

She was still crying. He touched her cheek and she raised to kiss him. He tried to put his arms around her, but he couldn't.

"I'm sorry," he said.

139

"It's all right now," she assured him. "It's over now."

"Is it?"

"You mean Al?"

"Yes. He must think he killed me."

"Maybe he won't come back here," she said.

"I hope not. I'm in no condition for a third round with him. I sure lost the first two."

"You're feeling better."

He nodded. "Tired. But I'm not woozy any more."

Cannon came into the room. "There are cops at our place," he said.

"How many?"

"One car."

"Go talk to them. You haven't done anything. Go talk to them."

"What if they want you?"

"Why should they want me?" He tried to laugh. "Go sell them some insurance."

Cannon went out and Stone heard him call, "Hey, are you looking for me?"

"Marianne," Stone said. "Help me get up."

"Stay where you are. You need to rest."

"What if they come here?"

"So you're sick. Stay there. You haven't done anything either except get shot."

"Stay with me?"

"All right." She sat down on the bed. She could see Fran and Sally. They were looking out the window.

Stone said, "Will you marry me?"

She looked at him and smiled. "Yes."

"Will you help me be a doctor?"

She kissed him on the forehead. "I'll force you to be a doctor." She smiled, but she raised up and looked toward the front. She looked frightened. "I wish Jack would get back," she said.

"He'll be back. Don't worry. How much of a sentence can they give me for getting shot?"

"Aren't you scared?"

"No."

"The police are coming here," Fran called.

140

Marianne started forward, but Cannon came into the trailer with two policemen. He shook his head and walked past the girls into the bedroom.

"What's going on?" Stone said.

"This is Burt Stone," Cannon said to the policemen. "He lives with us, too. He's got some kind of virus or something and he's not feeling too well. Miss Nirvell here is a nurse and she's sort of looking after him."

Sally Talent grabbed Cannon's arm. "What's happened?"

"Al's dead," Cannon said.

Sally said, "No, he's coming back here."

"He's dead!"

"What happened?" Stone asked, his voice quaking despite his attempt to control it.

"Do you know where he was tonight?" One of the policemen said.

"No. I haven't seen him tonight."

There wasn't any reason for them not to believe him. He was sick, they could tell that by looking at him. He was pale and the nurse said he had a fever. But they asked him the routine questions and then they left. There wasn't any case; the case was solved. The money was returned. The criminal was dead.

"He must have for sure figured you were dead," Cannon said when they were gone, "and he decided to do the job by himself. He got away from the store all right, but they picked up after the car because it was stolen. The cops told me they never saw anyone drive like that. The one cop said he would have just run away and left them eventually. Only he came up over a hill out there and some dumb ass of a truck driver was in the wrong lane, trying to pass another truck, and Al plowed into him."

"Killed him," Stone said.

"Crushed him," Cannon said. His voice cracked. "I got to go identify him."

Sally was crying and Fran had her arms around her, but Sally shoved them away and said, "You dirty yellow bastards, you let him down," and she went to the front and lay down on the couch.

Cannon turned and looked up through the trailer at Sally.

"I've got to identify him," he said. "I told them I'd come down."

CHAPTER 21

It was raining but they had perfect weather for the funeral. It didn't start raining until after they were home.

Jack Cannon walked into the living room of the trailer and put down his suitcase. "I'll see you, buddy," he said.

Stone said, "Why don't you stick around?"

"No. I think I'd better get on back up to Massillon. I think it's time. I've got Dad's business to get into up there. I don't have much here."

Marianne was on the couch beside Stone. She smiled at Cannon and said, "We'll come to see you."

"I'm counting on it." He held out his hand and Stone stood up and took it. "I want to be your best man," he said.

"Nobody else."

He and Stone looked at each other and Stone said, "We did what we could."

"We paid for the funeral."

"That's all we could do."

"Did you give the money to his mother?"

"Yes."

"Fran's down at the trailer," Marianne said. "You're not leaving without saying good-by to her, are you?"

"I'll go see her." He smiled. "Fran," he said.

"She likes you."

"I like her, too, but we don't love each other."

She smiled at him. "All right, but go see her. She'll want to say good-by."

"I'll see her again sometime." He turned to look at Stone. "Forget it now, buddy," he said.

"Sure. You, too."

They looked at each other and then Cannon picked up his suitcase. "So long now," he said. He stopped at the door and said, "Did you hear where Sally is?"

"No."

"I wonder where she is. I thought sure she'd be at the funeral."

"I don't know," Marianne said. "She was afraid they might be able to tie her to the robbery somehow since she was working at the store. Maybe she went to New York. She talked about going there. If they ever want her, I suppose they'll find her. But she was scared, so she ran."

Cannon nodded and he looked at Stone again. He hesitated, as if there were something he wanted to say, but he shoved open the door and went out.

Marianne said, "He's right."

"Right about what?"

"You have to forget it."

"Sure."

Cannon had put his suitcase into the car and Stone could see him walking toward the other trailer.

"Do you still want to marry me?" she said.

"Yes."

"Then I can tell you things, just like I'm your wife already."

"Okay."

"You forget about Al Leeds."

"It was my fault. Sally was right. I let him down." He looked at her. "It's my fault he's dead."

"No. The guilt was as much his as yours, but if you have guilt, you have to live with it."

"I know," he said.

"All right."

Guilt, she thought. *God, how it stays with us. But we have to live with it. I didn't want to hurt him. He wanted me to say that it wasn't his fault, but he wouldn't have believed me. I don't care how guilty he is of Al Leeds' death. I love him. But he doesn't know yet how guilt works, how it numbs and fades until it's not there very often, until there's not much of it left. That's all we can hope for. We can't live without being guilty of something. But we help each other. He helped me without even knowing about my guilt. Just loving him helps and it will help him to love me.*

"You'll be a doctor," she said.

"If you help me."

"We'll help each other."

"Let's get married right away," he said suddenly. "I don't want to wait."

"All right."

It's in his eyes, she thought. *I can see it there. I wonder if anyone can see my guilt in my eyes. I'll tell him about mine sometime, when it's particularly bad for him. I'll tell him what I know about guilt.*

Maybe it was his fault. What of it now? Part of the guilt was Al's, part Jack's, Sally's, mine. Even Fran. What of it? We all have to live anyway. Sometimes I think there are only two kinds of people, children, and the guilty.

It will make him a good doctor, but he doesn't know that yet. Maybe he won't ever realize it. I won't tell him that. He wouldn't believe it from me. If he ever learns it, he has to learn it for himself. I'll tell him that love and guilt aren't very different, that maybe that's what is meant by original sin. I'll tell him we're all guilty. All of us. We didn't have to do what we did, but I'll tell him that if we weren't guilty, maybe we wouldn't love each other. Maybe we couldn't . . .

"There goes Jack," he said. He watched the car. "I'll miss him."

"It's all right to miss Al, too," she said.

"What?"

"We have to live. Jack and you and Fran and Sally and I. It's all right for us to miss Al."

He nodded, but she didn't think he understood her. Not yet.

THE END